Buenos Aires Docs

Finding the prescription for a love that lasts...

Meet the dedicated medics of the
Hospital General de Buenos Aires. They might be
winners in their work, but they all need a little help
when it comes to finding their happy-ever-afters!

Luckily for them, passion is sweeping through the
corridors of the hospital like a virus and no one
is immune! Are they brave enough to take their
chance on happiness...and each other?

Find out in

Sebastián and Isabella's story
ER Doc's Miracle Triplets by Tina Beckett

Carlos and Sofia's story
Surgeon's Brooding Brazilian Rival by Luana DaRosa

Gabriel and Ana's story
Daring to Fall for the Single Dad by Becky Wicks

Felipe and Emilia's story
Secretly Dating the Baby Doc by JC Harroway

All available now!

Dear Reader,

I hope you enjoy escaping to Buenos Aires in *Secretly Dating the Baby Doc* and following Emilia and Felipe on their love story journey. Their romance proves that love can strike at any age! As Felipe says, *Why should the youngsters have all the fun?*

Love,
JC

SECRETLY DATING THE BABY DOC

JC HARROWAY

H Harlequin

MEDICAL ROMANCE

Special thanks and acknowledgment are given to JC Harroway for her contribution to the Buenos Aires Docs miniseries.

Harlequin®
MEDICAL
ROMANCE

Recycling programs
for this product may
not exist in your area.

ISBN-13: 978-1-335-94245-6

Secretly Dating the Baby Doc

Harlequin Enterprises ULC
22 Adelaide St. West, 41st Floor
Toronto, Ontario M5H 4E3, Canada
www.Harlequin.com

Printed in U.S.A.

Lifelong romance addict **JC Harroway** took a break from her career as a junior doctor to raise a family and found her calling as a Harlequin author instead. She now lives in New Zealand and finds that writing feeds her very real obsession with happy endings and the endorphin rush they create. You can follow her at jcharroway.com and on Facebook, Twitter and Instagram.

Books by JC Harroway

Harlequin Medical Romance

A Sydney Central Reunion

Phoebe's Baby Bombshell

Gulf Harbour ER

Tempted by the Rebel Surgeon
Breaking the Single Mom's Rules

Forbidden Fling with Dr. Right
How to Resist the Single Dad
Her Secret Valentine's Baby
Nurse's Secret Royal Fling

Visit the Author Profile page
at Harlequin.com for more titles.

To all the moms, working mothers and
single parents—great job!

CHAPTER ONE

Consultant neonatal surgeon Emilia Gonzales strode along the indistinguishable hospital corridor, her head held high as if she knew exactly where she was going. No one would guess it was her first day—new job, new hospital, new country.

Battling nerves and a raft of other unsettling emotions, she followed the signs for Theatre, scanned her security pass and entered the operating suite. Faced with another corridor, she tried to orientate herself to her surroundings.

She'd been given a tour when she'd come to the Hospital General de Buenos Aires for her interview earlier in the year. She was used to working in leading tertiary referral hospitals in her native Uruguay, but the General was four times the size of its counterpart in Montevideo. And she couldn't help but be distracted by the painful dull throb of her heart.

Her late husband, Ricardo, had been born in this very hospital. Despite five years of widowhood, Ricardo was always in her thoughts. How was she supposed to work here, be back here in Argentina, and not be constantly reminded of the loss of the love of her life?

Emilia breathed through the now familiar grief, pulling herself together. This new job represented a fresh start for her and her daughter, Eva. Eva had wanted to attend the same university as her father, and Emilia was happy to facilitate and support all of Eva's dreams. She just wished this particular change could be less triggering.

'Are you lost?' A man spoke from behind Emilia, making her jump.

She turned, and found herself eye to chest with his tall, athletic frame and looked up. With dark hair sprinkled with grey and deep brown eyes, her rescuer's friendly smile immediately set Emilia at ease.

'Is it that obvious?' she asked with a smile of her own. 'I was hoping to hide it better. It's my first day.' And she had a surgery to get to.

The tall and helpful stranger glanced at her brand-new name tag, his expression shifting from mild curiosity to pleasant surprise.

'Ah, you're Dr Gonzales,' he said, his smile widening. 'Our new neonatal surgeon. I've been expecting you.'

'Sorry if I'm late,' Emilia said with a wince. That was no way to make a good first impression.

'Not late at all.' He offered his hand. 'I'm Felipe Castillo. Welcome to the General.'

Emilia shook his hand, momentarily thrown by his welcoming manner and the confidence of his relaxed smile. They'd never met before, but she knew Felipe Castillo was a senior neonatal surgeon there. Not only was he jointly responsible for the patient Emilia was in Theatre to meet, he was also Emilia's clinical supervisor, until her full registration with the Argentine Medical Council was granted.

'Please, call me Emilia,' she said, sliding her hand from Felipe's warm and sure grip, her nerves intensifying.

They were a similar age, both in their fifties, but Felipe would be overseeing all her surgeries for a probationary period of three weeks. As a mother, Emilia had taken a little longer to train, what with maternity leave, years of part-time work while Eva had been small and then time off on compassionate leave during the two years Ricardo had been ill.

Only she hadn't expected her clinical supervisor to be so…attractive—setting her heart aflutter and raising her body temperature. After losing Ricardo, she'd assumed herself immune to physical desire, but no, her body seemed to be fully back in business. Her stare furtively dipped to his left hand, confirming the absence of a wedding ring, but his marital status was irrelevant.

As she'd told Eva again and again, she wasn't interested in dating. It seemed too hard and pointless as well. She'd had the great love of her life, and she had no intention of looking for love again.

'I'm looking for Theatre Six, the Lopez case,' she said. 'I assume that's where you're heading, too, seeing as we're going to be working together for a few weeks.'

'I am.' Felipe nodded and gestured with an outstretched arm. 'Allow me to show you the way.'

Emilia gratefully fell into step at his side, ignoring the sexy surgeon's swagger and how good he looked in the hospital's shapeless, green scrubs. She rarely noticed a member of the opposite sex, but when she did it still somehow felt as if she were cheating on Ricardo.

But then, they had been married for over twenty years. Sometimes, when she remembered that he was gone, she had to catch herself. It was as if half her heart was missing.

'So you're from Uruguay?' Felipe asked, glancing her way with obvious interest. 'What brings you to Buenos Aires?'

Emilia sucked in a breath. She'd known this line of questioning was inevitable. Consultants her age, the wrong side of fifty, rarely shifted hospitals, unless it was for personal reasons. And there was nothing more personal to Emilia than her beloved daughter, Eva.

'My late husband was Argentine. He was born in this hospital in fact,' she said, her voice tight. It often was when she talked about Ricardo. 'Our daughter wanted to go to university here, so I thought I'd make the move, too, as it's just the two of us. My parents died a few years ago, so there's no family keeping me in Uruguay.'

She trailed off, aware that she might be viewed as an over-protective mother. She had no intention of smothering Eva, but her eighteen-year-old daughter was all the family Emilia had left. It made sense to at least reside in the same country in case of emergencies, and to emotionally support Eva.

But she was thrilled that Eva would be able to spend more time with her father's side of the family. Losing her father at the age of thirteen, Eva had been through a lot. There'd been times during the past five years where Emilia had worried for her daughter's mental health—she'd seemed so sad and withdrawn.

'And why not?' Felipe's easy smile widened. 'Why should the youngsters have all the fun?'

'Quite.' Emilia heard herself laugh, the sound high pitched and a little strained. Since Ricardo's death, there'd been little time and even less inclination for *fun*. What with raising a teenager solo and maintaining her busy and demanding career, Emilia often reached the end of another week exhausted and faced with the realisation that, yet again, she'd inadvertently put herself last.

'Buenos Aires is a great city,' Felipe continued, with enthusiasm. 'You'll both love it here, I'm sure, once you've settled in.'

Emilia stayed silent. Settling into a new life, a new home and new job would be no mean feat. But as long as Eva was happy, she'd be happy.

Just as they rounded the corner to Theatre Six, their pagers sounded in unison with an urgent call.

'Looks like we made it in the nick of time,' Felipe said, silencing the alarm.

They hurried into Theatre Six's scrub room and passed their pagers to a theatre technician. Felipe reached for a theatre hat and mask and Emilia did the same.

'Nothing like a little excitement to start your first day,' he added, switching on the water over the sinks and vigorously washing his hands.

Emilia laughed. 'If you say so.'

Tamping down her adrenaline with some deep breaths, she glanced into the theatre as she joined him at the sinks. Through the glass, they had a bird's eye view of the brightly lit obstetrics' theatre. Isabella Lopez was already gowned up and surrounded by the delivery team, and a man Emilia assumed was Sebastian Lopez, her husband.

'So, a few weeks ago, the smallest of the Lopez triplets was prenatally diagnosed with a congenital diaphragmatic hernia, using foetal MRI scanning,' Felipe said, bringing her up to speed on the case as they scrubbed up, side by side.

Emilia nodded, working a scrubbing brush under her nails. 'I came in early to read the case file. I understand you performed a fetoscopic endoluminal tracheal occlusion at twenty-seven weeks. That's impressive in a multiple pregnancy.'

He raised his eyebrows over his mask. 'You'll see I'm not a shy surgeon. But the parents, Isabella and Sebastian, are both emergency doctors here at the General, so they were happy to consider the procedure. They want the best possible outcome for all three babies, so together we weighed the pros and cons of the FETO. Hopefully the gamble paid off.'

'I met Isabella Lopez when I came for my interview in January,' Emilia said, briskly scrubbing her hands and arms.

She'd immediately clicked with the other woman, who, along with her husband, ran the emergency department at the General. And after their difficult fertility journey, she knew how much the couple wanted these three miracle babies that were about to be born. At nearly

thirty-one weeks gestation, all three Lopez triplets would need to spend some time on the neonatal intensive care unit, or NICU, and the smallest
baby also faced surgery to correct the defect in
the diaphragm.

'Right, let's go meet the Lopez triplets,' Felipe
said, turning off the taps and using his back to
push through the door into the operating room.

Three resuscitation tables for newborns were
set up to one side of the room, each warmed and
awaiting a baby. A cluster of neonatal registrars
and nurses waited nearby, expressions tense.

Emilia glanced over at Isabella, trying to send
her calming positive vibes from behind her mask.
The birth of a child was always emotional, but
when the babies were premature and one needed
surgery, it might be overwhelming for the couple.

After being assisted by scrub nurses into surgical gowns and sterile gloves, Felipe and Emilia
nodded to the Lopezes and joined the obstetrician
performing the elective caesarean section.

The first two babies were delivered, one after
another. Their umbilical cords were clamped, and
they were quickly whisked away by the neonatal
team. Each baby was placed on the resuscitation
table's heated mattress. The neonatal nurses gently dried the newborns with a towel and cleared
their noses of mucus with a small suction tube.

'Apgar is nine,' the registrar caring for the first triplet said.

Emilia breathed a sigh of relief and glanced at Felipe, who nodded. The oldest Lopez baby had a low birth weight but was breathing spontaneously, had a good skin colour and normal reflexes, his condition stable enough for transfer to the NICU. The baby was wrapped up and carried over to Mamá and Papá for a quick cuddle.

At the next resuscitation table, triplet number two was being assessed by a second registrar. While slightly smaller than his brother, baby two was mewling loudly, his tiny pink face scrunched up in outrage.

'Apgar is ten,' the neonatal nurse said, wrapping him in a sheet and scooping him up for a few seconds of skin-to-skin contact with his parents.

Emilia smiled under her mask at Isabella and Sebastian's joy. But there was still one more baby to deliver. As the obstetrician delivered the head of the third and smallest baby, the atmosphere in the room changed.

'Syringe,' Felipe asked, holding out his hand.

The tube blocking the baby's airway, which had kept the lung expanded as the baby developed in utero, needed to be removed before the umbilical cord was cut, as it was essentially breathing for the baby via the placenta.

Emilia had only seen the FETO procedure a

handful of times, so she was glad for Felipe's greater experience in this instance. Felipe quickly deflated the balloon and removed the endotracheal tube from the baby's mouth. The delivery of the third Lopez baby was completed and the cord clamped as usual. Except unlike his brothers, baby three was limp and silent, his skin grey with cyanosis—a lack of oxygen.

Moving quickly, Emilia and Felipe carried the baby to the third resuscitation table, which had been set up in a screened off area with dimmed lighting.

While a nurse suctioned mucous from the mouth and nose, Emilia gently dried the baby with a towel to stimulate spontaneous respiration. Urgency shunted her pulse through the roof. She reached for the neonatal resuscitator, just in case the third triplet failed to start breathing on his own.

Those couple of seconds, during which the baby made no respiratory effort, felt endless. Emilia willed him to make it, her stare flicking to Felipe's.

'There's a heartbeat,' Felipe said, removing his stethoscope, 'but little respiratory effort. We already know from the scans that the left lung is hypoplastic.'

Emilia nodded, quickly but gently inflating the baby's underdeveloped lungs with the resuscitator.

The third Lopez baby was struggling to breathe unaided. Because of the hole in the diaphragm, abdominal organs had herniated into the chest and prevented the left lung from growing. Felipe had mitigated some of the pressure on the developing lungs with the FETO procedure, but the underdeveloped lung was still smaller than normal.

Emilia placed electrodes on the newborn's chest, her relief mounting when the heart monitor picked up a normal trace.

Their eyes met over the tops of their masks. 'We still have sinus rhythm,' Emilia told him.

Felipe nodded, his thoughts likely matching hers. For the time being, the smallest Lopez baby would need to be ventilated until they could close the diaphragmatic defect and give his lungs the space to grow.

'I'm going to intubate,' Felipe said, reaching for a laryngoscope and endotracheal tube. 'Then we'll transfer him to the NICU.'

With the intubation complete, Emilia passed a nasogastric tube into the baby's stomach to empty it of any contents and take the pressure off the baby's tiny lungs, which were already compromised by the herniation of small bowel loops into the chest.

As the baby's oxygen saturations climbed into the normal range, Felipe inserted an umbilical vein catheter into the cord so they could administer fluids, drugs and easily take blood samples. They worked together as if they'd been doing it for years, each of them anticipating the other's moves and assisting where required.

Once they had the third triplet stabilised, Emilia glanced at Felipe. 'A quick hello to Mamá and Papá and then up to NICU?'

Felipe nodded, peeling off his gloves and mask. 'Let's reassess him this afternoon, but he's booked for surgery in two or three days, as long as he remains stable. The sooner we can close that hole in his diaphragm the better.'

As Isabella was still on the table being sewn up from her C-section, Felipe and Emilia carefully wheeled the mobile resuscitation table over to the parents.

'We knew from the scans that the left lung was small,' Felipe explained to Isabella and Sebastian, who were understandably tearful and overwhelmed, 'so I've placed baby three on a ventilator, to help him breathe.'

'We've decided to name him Luis,' Sebastian said, gently taking his wife's hand so together they could reach out and touch their son's tiny curled fist.

'We're taking Luis to the NICU,' Emilia said, trying to sound reassuring, although they all knew the situation was serious. 'As soon as you're ready, you can see him and his brothers there. Try not to worry.' She met Isabella's stare. 'We'll take the best of care of them.'

Isabella nodded, tears seeping from the corner of her eye as she reached out and squeezed Emilia's hand. From one mother to another, Emilia heard what was being left unsaid: *Take care of my babies while I can't*.

'Congratulations on the birth of your sons,' Felipe added, resting his hand on Sebastian's shoulder, as if he too was aware of the turmoil and concern of the new parents. 'What a blessing.'

While the registrar and neonatal nurses whisked Luis upstairs to the NICU, Felipe and Emilia degowned, tossing the garments into a dirty laundry bin outside Theatre Six.

Emilia sagged a little, releasing an audible sigh as most of the adrenaline left her system. 'Well, that *was* an eventful first morning.'

Felipe nodded, one side of his mouth curling up in a charming smile. 'Now that the excitement is over, let me show you the most important room in the department, in case you get lost again.'

Emilia ignored the return of the silly flutter in her chest at how attractive and charming he was. It made no difference. That Felipe was so friendly and welcoming was nice, given they'd be working so closely together, but it also left her strangely unsettled. She wasn't used to male attention, not that he was overtly flirting. Would she even know what flirting looked like, having been off the market for so long?

'I hope it's the coffee room.' She laughed, smoothing her hat-flattened hair back from her face. 'I may not know my way around the rest of the hospital yet, but when I came for my interview, I made sure to ask for directions to the nearest coffee machine.'

'A woman with priorities,' he said with that confident smile that put her at ease, but also sped up her pulse. 'Although there's only instant in the break room. For the real thing, espresso, the best place to go is Café Rivas, upstairs in the foyer.'

'Oh, I definitely need the real thing to get through my first day.' Instant coffee just wasn't going to cut it.

'In that case,' he said, 'why don't I show you the way?'

'Great, thanks.' She followed him from the suite of theatres and up the stairs. She'd have to find her way around the hospital without his help soon enough. But, for now, there was no harm in accepting a guided tour from a supportive and approachable colleague.

'Café Rivas has an app so you can pre-order drinks without waiting in line,' he said, pushing through double doors at the top of the stairs.

'Uh-oh,' she said, waggling her eyebrows, 'that sounds dangerous.'

'Very,' Felipe agreed, holding the door open for her to pass through. 'Although I won't tell if you don't. It will be our little secret.'

Emilia couldn't help but smile, even as she felt her barriers rising. Charming, a fearless surgeon and hot. Never mind the easily accessible coffee being dangerous—she'd have to be very careful around Felipe Castillo.

CHAPTER TWO

FELIPE OFTEN HEADED to Café Rivas for a fix before a routine Theatre list. But with Emilia's fascinating company, there seemed to be an extra spring in his step today that was in no way related to the promise of caffeine.

'So what can I get you?' he asked as they entered the sun-filled café, which was situated at the front of the main hospital foyer and serviced both staff and visitors alike.

'A cappuccino,' she said, 'but *I* can get it.'

'Please, allow me,' he insisted, noticing the appealing slope of her exposed neck and the rich brown of her tied-back hair. 'Until you've had a chance to download the app,' he pressed, hoping to convince her. 'That way we can bypass the queue at the till.'

That the new neonatal surgeon was so stunning had caught him completely off guard. The hospital scrubs were forest green, a colour that complimented her skin tone and the golden brown of her eyes. As standard issue, they weren't that flattering, but he didn't need to be medically qualified to know her slender athletic build ticked every box for him. She was exactly his type.

'Okay, thanks,' she said. 'I owe you one.'

Felipe inclined his head, hoping there'd be plenty of opportunities to share drinks in their future.

'So, I realise that I bombarded you with questions earlier,' he said as they loitered near the espresso machine. 'Now it's your turn to ask me anything while we wait.'

'Okay…' She smiled, her studied observation raising his body temperature a few degrees.

'What drew you to neonatal surgery?' she asked. 'Do you have your own children?'

'No, I don't.' Felipe shook his head, loving her directness—a woman who knew her own mind. She didn't strike him as someone who would play games. And after fifteen years of casually dating, Felipe had seen every game in the book.

'Luckily I love kids,' he continued, 'given our work. I just never quite got around to having one of my own. My ex-wife didn't want children, and I was content to see them every day here.'

He shrugged, thinking of his younger brother, Thiago, and Castillo Estates, the family vineyard business that Felipe had refused to take over in favour of selfishly pursuing his medical career. Now that Felipe was committed to staying single,

and had just turned fifty-five, the burden of pro-
ducing the next generation of Castillo children
was solely down to Thiago and his soon-to-be
wife, Violetta.

The same single-mindedness that had driven
Felipe to pursue his own profession had probably also led him to neglect his marriage, while he
worked to prove to his family that he'd made the
right decision in pursuing medicine. Not that his
divorce was solely his fault…

'How about you?' he asked, shoving his ex-wife
of fifteen years, Delfina, from his mind. 'Just the
one daughter?'

He'd rather talk about the fascinating and sexy
new consultant than think about his failed marriage. Or how he'd also let down both his brother
and his parents. Emilia Gonzales was surprisingly
down to earth, clearly intelligent and utterly gorgeous. He couldn't help but wonder if she was
seeing anyone…

'Yes, Eva.' Emilia smiled, maternal pride shining in her eyes. 'She's just started law at UBA.'
Her smile deepened to reveal a charming dimple
in one cheek.

'Not medicine?' he asked, surprised. 'The University of Buenos Aeries has an excellent medical
school. That's where I trained.'

Emilia laughed, shaking her head so her pony-
tail swung. 'No—I managed to somehow put her

off. Instead, she's following in her father's footsteps. He studied law at UBA, too.'

Felipe could instantly tell that she and Eva were close. No wonder she'd made the shift to Buenos Aires when her daughter moved there to study. But starting over in your fifties could be…isolating.

'Eva sounds scarily smart,' he said, newly intrigued by the woman with whom, at first glance, he had heaps in common.

'Oh, she is,' she agreed, tilting her head to observe him in a way that saw him clenching his abs.

Now he was grateful that he worked hard to keep in shape. There was obviously a spark between them, a mutual attraction.

'So, how long have you been divorced?' she asked.

'Fifteen years,' he confessed, wincing when her eyebrows shot up with surprise. 'It was a perfectly amicable split,' he continued, feeling, as he always did, that he needed to justify his divorce. 'We'd just drifted apart.'

And over those fifteen years, he'd carved out a great life for himself, finding the perfect balance of work and social life, punctuated by the occasional casual date. Only no matter how many years passed, he couldn't seem to shake off the guilt that, because he'd pursued his career so diligently, he'd been a second-rate husband. No wonder he was content to date casually. Unlike Thiago, who was about to walk down the aisle.

Emilia eyed him a little more closely, as if trying to figure him out. 'Do you have a new partner?'

It was a logical next question, but he couldn't help hearing a hopeful curiosity in her voice.

'No, I'm single. I date, but nothing serious. What about you? Do you mind me asking how long it's been since your husband died?'

The curiosity was mutual. If she was on the market, he'd definitely be interested in something casual.

'Ricardo,' she said, supplying her husband's name as pain dulled her stare for a second. 'He's been gone five years.'

'I'm sorry.' Why had he asked? They'd only just met and now he'd made her sad. 'Starting again at our age is an adjustment,' he added, trying to repair the damage, 'and that's without moving to a new country the way you have.'

It was difficult enough to meet new people, especially the *right* people. He knew. He'd had fifteen years of experience.

'Oh, I'm not starting again apart from this new job.' She self-consciously toyed with her long hair, avoiding his stare. 'I'm too focused on making sure that Eva is settled here to worry about myself.'

Felipe's stomach fell. So she *wasn't* dating. He could understand why she put her daughter's needs above her own. Her situation was very different from his. She'd clearly loved her husband to the end, and probably still did. That didn't mean she was immune to loneliness though, especially given that her daughter was all grown up and would presumably be leaving the nest one day soon.

Maybe they could simply be friends?

'Well, there's no shortage of things to do in Buenos Aires,' he said, hiding his disappointment that he couldn't ask her out. 'What do you like to do when you're not working?'

Although given that he had to supervise her surgeries and make a report to the Argentine Medical Council, it was probably for the best that she was off limits. He didn't want Emilia to be at the centre of any hospital gossip.

'Gardening, reading, walks in the park with the dog. Nothing exciting.' She laughed. 'I get all the adrenaline I need from work.'

Felipe chuckled in agreement. Everything about her so far was seriously attractive.

'What about you?' she asked, watching him again.

'The same, actually, minus the gardening. I live

in an apartment, and I usually *run* in the park with the dog. He's a border terrier. Dante.'

Excitement lit her eyes. 'Mine's a springer spaniel—Luna. Although she's really my daughter's dog, I always seem to be one doing the walking...'

'Funny that,' he grinned, knowingly. 'So do you know anyone here in Buenos Aires?'

Emilia shook her head, a slight flush to her cheeks. 'No. My husband's family are from Córdoba.'

'In that case, we should get the dogs together sometime for a doggy date at the park.' Felipe held up his hands. 'That's not a line, just a friendly invitation.'

Emilia offered him a watery smile, failing to hide her horror at the idea.

Before she could politely decline, he jumped in. 'But I'm sure you'll have no trouble finding the best dog parks in the city without my help.'

He'd heard the message—she *really* wasn't interested. Just then, the barista called out Felipe's name and held out their takeaway order.

'Here you go,' Felipe said, passing Emilia her coffee.

'Thanks,' she said, heading with him towards the exit. 'I'm going to meet my registrar on the NICU and do a quick ward round, acquaint myself with the patients I've inherited from my pre-decessor.'

They paused at the top of the stairs where he'd be heading down to Theatres, while she went up to the third floor.

'Page me if you need any help,' Felipe said. 'I'll see you back in Theatre. We have a full list this afternoon.'

Before they could part ways, Emilia touched his arm, stalling him.

'Sorry about just now, Felipe,' she said, look-ing mildly embarrassed. 'I'm just a little sensi-tive about the whole dating thing. Eva thinks it's high time I got back out there and I'm really not keen. It's something of a touchy subject at home.'

She'd just moved to a new country, a place that must hold painful memories of her husband. That would make anyone feel bewildered and reluc-tant to date.

'No need for an apology.' Empathy tightened Felipe's chest that they had yet another thing in common. 'I understand the well-meaning pres-sure from family. My younger brother is soon to be married, and my entire family think I too should remarry before it's too late.' He widened his eyes, mock horrified, and she smiled. He knew all was forgiven.

'I'm glad I'm not the only one being...*encour-*

aged.' She rolled her eyes. 'At our age, we can't possibly look after ourselves, can we?'

'One of the best things that comes with reaching half a century is that we know our own minds, right? You'll date when you're ready.' He shrugged. 'Or not.'

'I agree.' She smiled, gratitude sparkling in her eyes. 'But try telling that to my teenage daughter.'

They parted ways and Felipe headed downstairs, his spirits a little deflated. So he'd imagined the way she'd checked him out. Mistaken her friendliness for flirtation.

They could still be friends, though.

Except the dull throb of disappointment stayed with him for the rest of the day.

CHAPTER THREE

THAT NIGHT, AFTER a busy first day, Emilia and Eva met at an authentic Argentinian restaurant near the hospital. Eva ordered some sweet-sounding cocktail and shot her mother a familiar glare.

'You're too set in your ways, Mamá. You should try something new. We're celebrating the start of our new life.'

'You're right.' Emilia nodded, feeling a hundred years old. Part of her wished that she didn't need to start a new life. She'd liked her *old* life, when it had been the three of them: Ricardo, her and Eva. Starting over seemed monumental, not that she'd ever confess as much to Eva.

Emilia offered the server an apologetic smile. 'Actually, cancel the Chardonnay and make that *two* pomegranate gin fizzes, please.'

Trying new things kept life interesting, that's what she and Ricardo had always taught Eva. It was just that, for Emilia, *everything* in her life at the moment seemed new and mildly terrifying. New home that Ricardo hadn't ever lived in.

New job in a place with bittersweet reminders at every turn. New pressures to put herself back out there—on the *meat market*.

She hid a shudder. Now wasn't the time to dampen the mood by voicing her unpopular reflections.

'It sounds delicious,' she said to Eva as the waiter left. At least this concession over a drink was easier to grant than the ongoing battle over how long was too long to grieve for her husband.

'So how was your first day at work?' Eva asked, pushing her long brown hair over her shoulder.

Her dark eyes were so like Ricardo's that sometimes it hurt Emilia to look at her beautiful daughter.

'It was good,' she said, brightly. 'Busy and eventful. We had newborn triplets admitted to the NICU today.'

Eva's eyes rounded with empathy. 'Oh, I hope they'll be okay.'

'So do I.' Emilia nodded, sharing Eva's sentiment. She'd spoken to Isabella and Sebastian Lopez on the NICU before she'd left the hospital that evening. They were understandably concerned about all three babies, but were putting on brave faces.

But thinking about the tiny Lopez babies brought to mind her sexy surgical colleague, Felipe Castillo. Another new thing to contend with, the shock reawakening of a badly timed and in-appropriate sexual attraction. Of course, it was just Emilia's luck that her supervising consultant would be hot, divorced and, with fifteen years' experience, an expert in casual dating.

Yes, he'd made her first day a little less daunt-ing with his easy camaraderie and professional support, but the undercurrents of attraction be-tween them had also set her alarm bells ringing. He was the first man she'd truly noticed in *that* way since Ricardo, and she wasn't certain she was ready yet to open that particular can of worms.

She'd loved her husband of twenty-one years. She loved him still, despite him losing his battle with grade four brain cancer. Even after five years alone, being attracted to another man felt…some-how disloyal. But, she had no intention of acting on that attraction.

That was why she'd freaked out when Felipe had suggested a harmless walk in the dog park together…

What was wrong with her?

'How was university?' she asked Eva, chang-ing the subject.

'Good. It was clubs day,' Eva said, her eyes bright with excitement. 'I've signed up for social volleyball and the Modern Feminist's Society.'

'Sounds great.' Emilia's heart warmed that her daughter seemed to be embracing their new life much better than her mother. 'You'll soon be making more new friends.'

And Eva deserved a little happiness. After some rocky times over the past few years, when Eva had struggled with understandable bouts of sadness and anger over her father's untimely death, it was a relief to see her daughter energised about her university life.

'What about you?' Eva pressed. 'Did *you* meet anyone interesting at the hospital?'

Just then, the waiter returned with their drinks, placing the fussy pink concoctions on the table with a flourish.

'Of course not,' Emilia mumbled, a flush brewing, making her neck itchy. She pounced on her drink, taking a generous gulp to calm her nerves and hide her reaction from eagle-eyed Eva.

She didn't want to talk about Felipe Castillo and his confusing friendliness. She didn't want to examine her body's unexpected reaction to the man. She just wanted to feel like her old self, to remember that she was here in Buenos Aires primarily for Eva. She was focused on her daughter's happiness, rather than probing the soft, vulnerable spots of her own emotional and physical well-being.

Eva regarded her mother with suspicion. 'I hope you're not walking around with your eyes closed, Mamá. In a hospital as big as the General, there must be at least *one* single man your age.'

'I'm sure there is,' Emilia said, picking up the menu and scanning the delicious-sounding dishes, rather than thinking about the sexy, talented Felipe again.

Only everything was blurry—she needed her glasses.

'So…what are you having?' she asked, steering the conversation back to the menu. 'They have empanada, which look good.' Emilia fished around for her glasses from the bottom of her bag, aware of the loaded silence. She looked up to find Eva watching her with a clear and telling sympathy.

If she'd hoped to avoid this topic tonight, Emilia was out of luck.

'You know that Papá wouldn't want you to be alone forever, don't you?' Eva said, unfairly playing her winning argument.

Emilia had nowhere left to hide. She and Ricardo had even discussed this very situation, near the end, when it had become obvious that all treatment options had been exhausted. He'd made her promise to be happy. To take care of herself as well as their daughter.

But the execution of her promise wasn't straightforward. It meant overcoming her grief, being honest about her needs as a woman, stepping out of her comfort zone and putting herself out there into the terrifying ether of dating some…stranger.

Emilia blinked away the sting in her eyes and closed the menu in defeat. 'I know, I just…' Her throat tightened. She couldn't simply switch off her feelings for the man she'd loved most of her adult life. And deep down, what scared her most was that her dating again would be the final confirmation that Ricardo wasn't coming back.

Of course, she already knew that in her head, but her heart was much slower to adjust to this harsh new reality.

'*I* want you to be happy too,' Eva pressed, 'especially as we're starting over in a new country. I know I've encouraged you before, but perhaps now that we're here it's the perfect time to start dating.'

Would there ever be a perfect time for *that*? Emilia hadn't been single since her early twenties. Even if she wanted to get back out there, the rules of modern dating were a total mystery. There were apps and confusing terminologies. It was a steep learning curve.

'I'll think about it, okay?' She took another swallow of her overly sweet cocktail, hoping to put an end to the uncomfortable but familiar line of questioning. In desperation, Emilia scanned the restaurant's elegant and dimly lit booth-style layout for a glimpse of their server to take their order.

That was how she spotted Felipe Castillo a few tables away.

Emilia froze with shock.

He was casually dressed in dark chinos, a blue shirt open at the collar and a linen sports jacket. He looked cool and sophisticated—and he was pulling out a chair for a beautiful, statuesque brunette woman.

Emilia's body flooded with uncomfortable heat.

He was on a date, while she sat there mooning over how nice he'd been, making excuses for why she could never be interested in him, or any man, even casually. She made a crestfallen squawking sound in her throat. As if he'd heard her from across the room, he looked up and their eyes met.

The full body flush turned anticipatory. He looked so dashing in his regular clothes. More approachable, taller, hotter. It wasn't fair. They smiled at each other, then Emilia ducked her head, but not before she saw him murmur something to his date, who smiled up adoringly and touched his arm as he left her side.

'Oh, no…' Emilia whispered under her breath as she saw him head their way in her peripheral vision.

He was coming over. Now she'd have to act natural in front of Eva. She'd have to contain her surprise at how good he looked out of scrubs, *and* manage her disappointment that, despite what he'd told her in the hospital café, he was obviously taken.

But of course he was, a man like him…

She scrabbled for the menu again, opening it blindly while she tried in vain to control her blush.

Eva looked around, her eyes wide with curiosity. 'Who's that?' she whispered.

Emilia grimaced, her cheeks flaming. 'Just a colleague from the hospital.' She'd barely uttered the words when Felipe arrived at their table.

'Emilia. Good to see you,' he said, his smile wide and genuine, as if they were already old friends. 'I see you've discovered Buenos Aires's best kept secret. The tamales here are delicious.'

Emilia laughed nervously, pushing her reading glasses up on the top of her head so he came back into focus.

'Felipe,' she said, her voice emerging embarrassingly high pitched, 'this is the daughter I was telling you about, Eva.' She glanced at her delighted daughter, reluctantly completing the introduction. 'Felipe Castillo is a senior neonatal surgeon at the General. We're working together.'

Eva held out her hand and Felipe shook it with another warm smile.

'So you're the scarily smart law student,' he said.

Eva accepted the compliment with a shrug for Felipe and an intrigued glare for Emilia.

'I was telling your mum about the dog park in the city,' Felipe continued, easily charming Eva. 'It's a great place to take Luna. There's a pond and an obstacle course. My dog loves it.'

'Oh, thanks,' Eva said. 'I'll have to check it out, although Mamá loves to walk Luna, too.' She stared at Emilia, her excited eyes practically on stalks. 'Perhaps you could give her and Luna a tour sometime,' she added to Felipe.

Emilia glanced up at Felipe, apologetically, while inside she curled in upon herself with embarrassment. 'Felipe and I have already discussed that, Eva.'

Her face flamed as she turned to Felipe. 'But we won't keep you from your *date*.' She stumbled clumsily over the last word as if she didn't even want to say it, let alone *do* it. 'Thanks for the menu recommendation and enjoy your evening.'

'You too,' he said with an easy-going shrug. 'See you at work tomorrow. Eva, it was a pleasure meeting you.' With another devastating smile for Emilia, he made his way back to his table, to the woman who watched him approach with obvious adoration.

Emilia lowered her gaze to the tablecloth. She didn't want to witness Felipe sharing a romantic dinner with his glamorous date. Slowly, she exhaled the breath she'd been holding, an unexpectedly hollow sensation in her chest. But of course he was taken. He was single and hot, in or out of the scrubs, and a surgeon. Plus he had that smile thing going on, the one that came from his eyes and made you feel like the only person in the room…

Except she hadn't anticipated seeing him with another woman to trigger such an intense return of her loneliness. Maybe Eva was right; maybe she *did* need to address the gaping hole in her personal life. She didn't want to turn into one of those older women who lived only through their grown-up child.

Eva deserved better than to have to worry about her poor sad Mamá.

'I thought you said you didn't meet anyone interesting at work today,' Eva said, dragging Emilia back into conversation. 'You two seem to have really hit it off.'

If only she could share Eva's obvious excitement. If only it was as simple as meeting a sexy man at work—one she had heaps in common with—and enjoying a few easy, confidence-building dates, nothing serious.

'Oh…? Not really,' Emilia bluffed, recalling how effortless and relaxed her and Felipe's few conversations had been, until she'd freaked out. 'I was lost on my way to Theatre this morning and he showed me the way.'

Her explanation fell flat, dragged down by her

dampened spirits. Fifty-two was no age to abandon companionship, even sex, altogether. Maybe she was overcomplicating the issue simply because she was terrified of taking the first step—a date with a man she'd never met.

'*And* he remembered your daughter's degree and the name of your dog,' Eva pointed out. 'He's obviously interested in *you*.' Her eighteen-year-old rolled her eyes as if Emilia was utterly clueless. And she wasn't wrong. Unlike Felipe, who'd been single and dating for fifteen years, Emilia was seriously out of practice.

She flushed at the very idea of Felipe Castillo finding her sexually attractive. Perhaps he also simply needed companionship, someone to laugh with, to enjoy a meal or a movie with. Maybe what Emilia needed the most was someone to remind her that, after the death of a beloved spouse, life went on.

Only one look at him all dressed up and smelling delicious, the way his date drooled at him, and instinct told her that Felipe's night was going to end with some pretty steamy sex.

'I don't think so,' she said, primly sliding on her glasses again so she could study the menu in earnest. She needed to stop thinking about Felipe Castillo's sex life. 'Anyway, he's obviously taken. In case you haven't noticed, he's on a date with a beautiful woman. He was just being polite.'

Eva scoffed. 'A date he abandoned to come over and say hello to *you*.' Then her expression softened with another of those sympathetic looks that made Emilia wince. 'But I'm sorry that he's taken. He seemed really nice, and you two obviously have heaps in common. You know what they say, though—*plenty more fish in the sea*.'

'No need to be sorry.' Emilia shooed away her daughter's well-meaning concern. 'I'm fine. I'm too busy with work and settling into our new life here, making sure you have everything you need, to worry about meeting men.'

'Mamá… What about what *you* need? Papá's been gone five years now.'

Emilia hid her sigh. As if she wasn't aware of every single one of the two thousand and eighty-six days she'd woken up without her husband, her best friend, her rock.

Eva reached for Emilia's hand across the table. 'I saw the way you smiled at Felipe. I think it's time you at least consider dating. Please… For me?'

Emilia winced, powerless in the face of her daughter's pleading. 'Okay, fine. I'll consider it.'

'Great.' Eva reached for Emilia's phone, scooping it up from the table.

'What are you doing?' Emilia spied the waiter heading their way and sagged with relief. If they passed on starters and dessert, they could be out of here in under an hour, and that way they'd avoid watching Felipe's romantic date unfold.

'I'm signing you up to a dating app,' Eva said with a stubborn expression. 'There are specific ones for the over forties, so you should have no problem finding someone you have things in common with.'

'Yay…' Emilia said sarcastically, surreptitiously glancing Felipe's way as he and the brunette clinked wine glasses in a toast.

'This is how you meet people these days, Mamá. You have to move with the times.'

Emilia smiled at her daughter, silently addressing her beloved Ricardo in her head: *Why, oh, why is our daughter so headstrong? And why did you have to go and leave me to this utterly daunting fate?*

CHAPTER FOUR

EARLY THE NEXT morning Felipe entered Café
Rivas and instantly spied Emilia waiting in the
coffee queue near the espresso machine.

His pulse galloped with the kind of excitement
that had been totally lacking from his date the
night before. Emilia looked sensational, smartly
dressed in a grey blouse and black skirt, her hair
clipped back at the nape of her neck and small
gold hoops in her ears.

What was it about her simple, sophisticated el-
egance he found so appealing? Was it just that
they had so much in common? That he admired
her intelligence and sense of humour? She even
had an obviously close relationship with her de-
lightful daughter, and it couldn't have been easy
raising a teenager alone.

She was so intent on her phone that she didn't
notice him approach.

'Did you enjoy your meal last night?' he asked,
startling her so she placed one hand over her heart
and laughed up at him with shock.

'Oh… Hi. Yes. It was delicious, thanks.' She pushed her glasses up onto her head the way she had last night. 'Eva wanted us to celebrate the first proper day of our *new life*.'

'Eva has her priorities set right, I think. Casa Comiendo is one of my favourite restaurants.'

She tucked the phone into the pocket of her skirt, a sheepish look on her face.

'Are you having trouble with the coffee app?' he asked. 'I'd be happy to help you set up a standing order for your favourite drink if you want. Cappuccino, right?'

'No… I, um…' She flushed prettily, glancing away so he noticed the berry-coloured sheen of gloss on her full lips. 'Well, the truth is, Eva signed me up to a dating app last night, and I was trying to turn off the notifications. My profile has only been live for fourteen hours and I keep getting hits or swipes or whatever they're called. It's very distracting and I have clinic this morning.'

Felipe's stomach took a disappointed dive, but he kept his smile fixed in place. So she *was* dating?

'I'm sure it shows,' she said, inclining her head in his direction and lowering her voice, 'but it's my first time on a dating app. I had no idea it would be so…overwhelming.'

Another wave of disappointment struck. No wonder her phone was going nuts. She was gorgeous and smart and sophisticated. She'd be beating men off with a stick. He swallowed the bitter taste in his mouth, wishing *he* could be the one to take her out and show her the best Buenos Aires had to offer. But he was supervising her. And her personal life—who she dated—was none of his business.

'If you want my advice, and I've been doing this for fifteen years,' he said, sticking his nose in because he felt somehow protective of her, and she was looking up at him expectantly, 'is to take your time. You don't have to feel pressured to meet anyone unless it feels right.'

She'd been off the market for what, over twenty years? Things had changed in that time. He knew exactly how it felt to relearn all of the dating rules.

At her relieved smile, a fresh surge of protective impulses shook him. Crazy. She was an intelligent grown woman with an adult child. She could take care of herself. Although they *were* colleagues, and she didn't yet have any friends in town…

She nodded, her brown eyes curious, as if she was appraising him every bit as much as he was her. 'Try telling Eva that. She seems to think that five years alone is long enough, which is why, despite my better judgement, I'm meeting some stranger called Santino tonight.' She stared at him, imploring. 'Help—what should I expect?'

Felipe stood a little taller, happy to take her under his wing, both in and out of the operating room.

'Things have certainly changed since we were in our twenties,' he said, trying not to think about this lovely woman with some lucky guy named *Santino*.

'Tell me about it.' She rolled her eyes and then sobered. 'I'm tempted to cancel, but I worry about Eva. She's been through a lot, losing her dad and now moving away from all her old friends. I don't want her to worry about *me*.'

Felipe nodded, his heart going out to her and her daughter. 'Well if you *do* meet this guy, make sure it's in a public place.'

She nodded intently, urging him to continue.

'A bar or a café is good, but not one that you frequent regularly,' he said. 'If you don't like him, or it doesn't work out, you don't want him showing up at your favourite haunts all the time.'

Emilia's eyes widened in horror. 'I didn't think of that, thanks.' She looked at him as if he'd just rescued her from a burning building. 'Anything else?'

Felipe fought the urge to tell her to forget other guys and date him instead, but he already felt invested in her happiness. 'It's better to suggest drinks rather than dinner for a first date. That way, if it's not going well, you can just cut the night short.'

'Another awesome tip,' she said, looking, if anything, a little *more* nervous.

'I'm sure it will be great,' he said, hoping to boost her confidence. If Santino had any sense, he'd realise what a great catch Emilia was and hold onto her, tightly. She was beautiful and intelligent. She had everything going for her.

She shrugged and then changed the subject. 'So, how was *your* evening last night?'

Felipe considered sugar coating it, but he didn't want to lie to her when she'd asked for his advice. 'Not great, to be honest.' He sighed, wishing he'd gone to his favourite restaurant alone last night. Who knew how the evening might have unfolded differently if he hadn't been on a date.

Her eyebrows rose with surprise.

'The food was delicious,' he said with a shrug, 'as it always is at Casa Comiendo. I ordered a world-class bottle of malbec—my family own a vineyard in Mendoza so I'm a bit of a wine snob, I'm afraid—but I won't be seeing my date again.'

Emilia paled a little. 'Oh…that bad, huh? I'm sorry.' Her expression was genuinely sympathetic, but he wanted to convince himself that he saw a flicker of excitement in her stare.

'Now I'm regretting the impulse to be brave and give dating a try myself,' she added with a wince.

'You have way more experience and there's still the possibility of failure. What hope do *I* have, a complete beginner…?'

'Don't be put off.' Felipe said, internally cursing fate that he was encouraging her to date other men when he was so attracted to her. 'I'm sure you'll have a great time.'

Why couldn't he meet someone like Emilia? Someone on his wavelength who wanted the same things—just some casual, fun dates. Although some instinct warned him that Emilia might only want that for now, but once recovered from her grief, she might one day want more.

'It's just that the trouble with dating apps,' he continued, 'is that someone can seem great on paper, but when you meet in person, you realise you have less in common that you thought.'

Emilia nodded vigorously. 'That's what worries me. I'd much rather meet someone the old-fashioned way. You know, face to face.'

'I agree.' Felipe nodded, thinking of how *they'd* met, instantly clicked, effortlessly got along.

'I'm not interested in commitment or marriage,' he continued, 'but no matter how many ways I make that clear on my profile, I still seem to attract women who want something serious after two dates.' Last night's second date had asked him *where this was going* over dessert.

'Hmm… That *is* tricky.' Emilia's lips twitched

playfully. 'I guess some women look at you and see the whole package—good job, tall, handsome...' she peered closer, mischief in her eyes '...your own teeth and hair.'

He laughed, shooting back, 'As opposed to someone else's.'

She chuckled and, once again, Felipe railed against the fact *Santino* had beat him to Emilia. She really was easy to talk to. Perhaps he should ask what app she was using and do a little swiping himself...

He sobered, dragging in a breath. 'I just wish people were honest about what they're looking for from the start. I have no time for game playing.'

Emilia tilted her head, regarding him thoughtfully. 'Maybe you'll meet someone at your brother's wedding. Apparently, weddings are, according to my daughter, a great place to meet people.'

'Yes...' he drawled sarcastically. 'Flirting with someone while my entire family eagerly looks on. Talk about overwhelming.'

She pressed those full lips of hers together, hiding a smile. 'Yes, I can see how that might be awkward. Poor you.'

Felipe grinned, decidedly pleased with himself that yet again their conversation was light and playful. Except she was going on a date with some other lucky guy.

'Have you reviewed Luis Lopez?' he asked,

changing the subject to one that didn't twist his gut with envy. He didn't want to think about some guy named Santino enjoying Emilia's sense of humour and her sparkling smiles. He definitely didn't want to think about her going home with the man…

'Yes,' she said, taking her takeaway coffee from the barista. 'I came in early and popped up to the NICU. He's stable. He's lost a little weight, but that's only to be expected. I spoke to Isabella and Sebastian again and they seem as happy as can be expected with the way things are going.'

Felipe's coffee arrived. He scooped it up and they left Café Rivas together.

'Do you want to review him together tomorrow morning?' he asked, pausing at a fork in the corridor as they were headed in opposite directions. 'First thing, before we take him to Theatre?'

He'd only known her a day, but it felt as if they'd been friends and colleagues for years. Except he couldn't ignore that unrelenting attraction…

'Sure,' she said taking a sip of her coffee and holding out her phone with her number displayed. 'Here's my number, text me when you arrive and I'll meet you on the NICU.'

Felipe stored her contact in his phone, an excited flutter in his gut. They had a date. A work date, but he'd take it.

'I'm on my way to the ED now,' he said. 'I'm on call today. Good luck tonight, with your date.'

'Thanks.' She winced. 'Somehow it feels like sitting an exam I haven't studied for.'

Forcing himself to step away from her easy and enchanting company, Felipe said, 'Just be yourself and you can't go wrong.'

She shot him a dubious look and walked off in the opposite direction.

He watched her depart for way too long. Why couldn't he meet a woman a bit more like Emilia Gonzales? Not exactly like her, because if her grief was any indication, she was obviously a lifelong commitment type, whereas he was a steadfast bachelor. Maybe the best plan of action was to forget his attraction to her and focus on their professional relationship—and what could be a highly rewarding friendship.

CHAPTER FIVE

THE NEXT DAY in Theatre, Emilia stood opposite Felipe while they operated together on tiny Luis Lopez.

Having met Isabella Lopez before the triplets were born, and now that she considered the younger woman a friend, she couldn't help her nerves. That Felipe was there helped boost her confidence as she gently guided the loops of small bowel through the defect in Luis Lopez's diaphragm, drawing them back into the baby's abdominal cavity.

Across the operating table, Felipe shifted his weight, his hand remaining steady on the small retractor, which held open the laparotomy incision in Luis's abdomen. Despite operating alone in Uruguay, she'd already grown used to Felipe's calming presence. Unsurprisingly, he treated her with respect, stepping back and merely observing to allow her to make the critical decisions. After only a couple of days at the General, she already felt like a valued member of the neonatal surgical team, and it was largely down to Felipe.

'Let's see what we're dealing with,' Felipe said, as Emilia exposed the two-centimetre hole in the baby's diaphragm.

'The scans measure the defect at twenty-eight percent,' she said, her mind weighing up the two possible surgical approaches. They could suture the defect closed, like sewing a hole in a jumper, or they could put a synthetic patch over the defect.

Felipe peered inside, assessing the situation. His stare met hers. 'Looks too big for a primary closure. Are you happy to patch the defect?'

'Yes, I think that's the best approach in this case,' she said, glad that he'd asked her opinion.

The scrub nurse opened the sterile synthetic patch and passed it to Emilia, who positioned it over the defect in the diaphragm. She'd only sutured half the patch in place when the heart monitor alarms sounded, shrilly disrupting the quiet.

Emilia paused what she was doing, her adrenaline spiking. All eyes turned to the anaesthetist.

'We have a bradycardia,' he said, while checking Luis's ventilation, oxygenation and blood pressure.

Emilia paused, her own heart rate frantic. Having her work there supervised, her every move and technique scrutinised, naturally led to a wobble of confidence. But she worked hard at her job, and she was good at it. There was no need to panic.

'Probably just a bit of vagal stimulation,' Felipe said, glancing at Emilia, encouragingly.

The vagus nerve innervated part of the diaphragm, so inadvertent irritation of the nerve during the surgical repair was the most likely explanation. Only Emilia wanted to be sure.

'I'm just going to thoroughly check for bleeding anyway.' She'd performed this procedure many times before in Uruguay, but never on a baby as small at Luis Lopez. She really appreciated Felipe's presence as a senior, more experienced surgeon.

'Are you happy for me to proceed?' she finally asked the anaesthetist after making her checks, taking in some deep breaths to slow down her own heart rate. The sooner they successfully completed the surgery, the happier she'd feel for baby Luis and his family.

At the anaesthetist's nod, Emilia continued suturing the synthetic patch over the hole in the diaphragm, the remaining surgery passing without a hitch.

'Would you like to close up?' she asked her registrar, who was close to sitting her final surgical exams and would soon be eligible for her own consultant post.

The younger woman nodded and swapped places with Emilia as Felipe did the same with his registrar. They would review Luis back on the

NICU. His recovery and prognosis would depend on his weight gain, lung development and the lack of both surgical and medical complications. For now, Emilia and Felipe had done all they could.

'There's a new admission to the NICU,' Felipe said, tossing his gloves and mask in the bin. 'A case of oesophageal atresia. Want to come and examine the baby with me? I'll probably add her to our Friday operating list.'

'Sure,' Emilia said, dumping her gown and hat into the used linen bin outside Theatre.

They washed up and headed up to the third floor together.

'Thanks for all your support back there,' she said, glancing his way. 'Before I moved here, I was nervous to be supervised, but I'm glad they chose *you* to oversee my work.'

Operating alongside Felipe had become second nature so quickly. They shared a similar surgical style, and Felipe was generous with his advice and knowledge, always looking out for her. It made her feel protected and valued, reminded her of how she'd felt the same within her marriage to Ricardo, who had always been her number one supporter, despite knowing nothing about medicine.

'You're welcome.' Felipe smiled at her compliment. 'I can understand your nerves. *I'd* feel the same. Speaking of nerves, how was your exam last night? Your date?'

She laughed at his joke and looked up at his

expectant face, searching for his feelings on the change of subject. Was he just being friendly, or was he genuinely interested in her sad dating life? But given that she'd asked for his dating tips, she was happy to share her experience.

'Honestly?' she asked, mentally comparing the man she'd met last night, Santino, to both Ricardo and Felipe, unfavourably so.

'Always the best policy,' Felipe said with a wince, as if already anticipating her bad news. He held open the door to the stairwell and Emilia passed through. He was such a gentleman.

'It was awful,' she confirmed, amused to see a hint of surprise in his expression, as if he'd truly been rooting for her. 'Right from the get-go,' she continued, warming to her horror story, 'I could tell all he wanted was for me to go home with him.'

Felipe scowled and Emilia nodded and went on. 'He wasn't interested in getting to know me at all. He clearly just wanted a hook up. So, it turns out that men play games, too.'

'I'm sorry that it didn't work out,' Felipe said, the excitement hovering in his eyes saying the opposite.

Emilia shrugged. She wasn't offended. She and Felipe obviously fancied each other. Eva was right… Oh, how it stung to admit that. But just because there was attraction didn't mean they should act on it. They were work colleagues. He was supervising her. She couldn't simply date him instead. She sighed, even more averse to the idea of dating now that she'd had a bad experience.

'I still need your advice,' she pleaded. 'You're my dating coach.'

He nodded, proudly, and Emilia continued. 'Blind dating seems fraught with potential disasters. How do I tell the good guys from the bad from their brief profiles?'

Felipe inclined his head in sympathy. 'I know it seems risky,' he said, obviously trying to make her feel better, 'but for every bad date there are a bunch of good ones. I promise you, next time will be better.'

He offered her that easy smile of his, the one that made him look approachable and trustworthy, and made her even more aware of how in sync they were. Emilia shook her head dubiously, wishing she'd trusted her instincts and stayed the hell away from the stupid dating app in the first place.

'I don't know if I have the patience for the bad ones though,' she said as they paused outside the NICU. 'Mr Horny—that's what I'm calling Santino—knocked back his drink in two swallows, offered to *walk me home*,' she made finger quotes, 'and when I refused, he made excuses and left. He'd pulled out his phone even before he'd walked away. Probably had another date lined up, just in case ours was a bust.'

'What a jerk,' Felipe said, his frown deepening as his stare traced her face.

He seemed genuinely outraged on her behalf, which was flattering. It was certainly nice to have an ally. For the first time in so long, she didn't feel quite as alone.

'Thanks for being on my side,' she said, smiling. If only there were plenty of Felipe Castillos out there. 'But I'm so out of practice with the whole dating thing that there's enough to consider without trying to figure out what the other person is thinking. At least you've had enough experience to know when it's worth persevering with someone. I've had *one* date and I'm just about ready to give up on the whole idea and delete my profile. If it wasn't for my promise to Eva, I would,' she added emphatically.

'I can totally see why you might feel that way.' He tilted his head, his deep brown eyes soft with empathy. 'Unless…'

His index finger tapped his lips in a way that made her acutely aware of their pleasing shape and apparent softness. 'Why don't *we* go out, strictly no strings.'

Emilia held her breath, her heart going crazy behind her ribs. Wasn't that exactly what she'd been thinking only moments ago? But they worked together. Was it a professional conflict? She didn't want to be the source of hospital gossip.

'I'll take you to another of my favourite restaurants,' he continued, enthusiastically, 'teach you all my top dating tips, and you can practice your dating small talk on me. It will give you a bit of confidence for the real thing.'

Emilia dithered, her stomach swooping excitedly. She already knew that five minutes of Felipe's easy and platonic company was worth at least ten excruciatingly awkward dates with horny strangers. Only there was that undercurrent of attraction to consider... Could she ignore that and simply enjoy his company? At least with Felipe there'd be no pressure to have a relationship. Like her, he just wasn't interested in anything serious.

But what would she tell Eva, who already thought Felipe fancied her?

'Oh...that sounds too good to be true,' she said, thinking how a casual date with Felipe under the guise of building up her confidence might actually appease her daughter. 'But we work together. Won't it be...awkward?'

Felipe shrugged his broad shoulders nonchalantly. 'Only if we have undeclared expectations.'

He glanced along the corridor as if making sure they were alone, and then dropped his voice. 'So you know exactly what you're getting with me, I'll come clean,' he said, casually folding his arms over his chest. 'I *do* find you attractive, but I also like you. We have a lot in common. I'd be happy to be just colleagues and friends, so it's just dinner. No games.'

Hearing his honest declaration seemed to light some kind of fuse inside her, the fizz and hiss of anticipation for their non-date date a hundred times greater than what she'd experienced during the real thing last night.

'I like you too,' she said, her throat tight with nervous energy and her cheeks warm, 'and we've already established that you're easy on the eye and in possession of your own hair and teeth.'

His delighted grin gave her courage.

'But if we *do* go out for dinner,' she added, 'that would be my second *date* in twenty plus years, so no-strings suits me just fine.'

She wasn't looking for a relationship. Her heart still belonged to Ricardo. But if she had to do this, put herself out there and get used to the idea that one day she might want to date for real, wasn't it better to practice with a man like Felipe? A man she knew and respected and had heaps in common with.

'Great,' he said, his eyes sparking with excitement. 'Then we're on the same page. You can try out your dating moves on me, knowing that I'm not trying to get you into bed, and I'll enjoy your company knowing that you're not hoping to move into my apartment by the weekend. We both win.'

His smile broadened and Emilia laughed, already looking forward to it. Perhaps she could wear that new dress in her wardrobe...

'I'll book us a table,' he said, 'and pick you up at seven tomorrow night. Does that work?'

'Seven it is,' she said with a smile, gently shaking her head.

He really was too self-assured for his own good. Some women couldn't help but find that irresistible. No wonder they fell for him hard. But Emilia wasn't looking to be one of those women. For one thing, they had a professional relationship to preserve, and for another she'd done her falling twenty-five years ago. Now she had other priorities, like building a stable life here in Buenos Aires for her and Eva.

'Only one more thing,' she said, pausing as they entered the NICU to meet their new oesophageal atresia patient, who'd been born earlier that morning. 'This stays just between us.'

'Of course.' He smiled, winked and paused at the sink to wash his hands.

Emilia joined him, slowly exhaling an excited breath.

A non-date date. Whatever would Eva think? But perhaps Emilia should keep it to herself. After all, it was only a practice date between two people uninterested in dating seriously. No use raising Eva's hopes unnecessarily.

CHAPTER SIX

THAT FRIDAY EVENING Felipe smiled across the table at Emilia and poured the last of the wine between their glasses. Unlike his last date, when most of the conversational burden had fallen to him, tonight's conversation had flowed non-stop from the minute he'd collected her from her neat two-bedroom house in a taxi.

He couldn't recall the last time he'd felt so excited by a new connection. Maybe it was because they were on the same page when it came to their relationship expectations, but he and Emilia seemed to just effortlessly click, the invigorating camaraderie they shared at work spilling over into their *date*. Except he needed to remember that it wasn't a *real* date, that they were just friends and colleagues.

'So what type of wine does your family's vineyard grow?' she asked, her deep brown eyes accented by the sapphire blue dress she wore, the neckline showing a tantalising glimpse of her tanned and freckled chest.

He was having a hard time keeping his stare from her sensational body. She looked elegant and relaxed, her make-up subtle and her long, dark hair swept over one tanned shoulder. Felipe forced his gaze away from the curve of her lovely lips back up to her playful stare. She really was stunning. And intelligent and interesting.

And a *friend*…

'We specialise in Syrah and Malbec, of course,' he said, naming the most famous of the Argentinian grape varieties, 'but we also grow Chardonnay and Semillon. My parents are retired now, so my brother has taken over and also added a sparkling wine to the estate's production line.'

'Ooh…' Emilia said, impressed. 'Do they have an open cellar door? I might have to visit the region sometime. I haven't been to Mendoza since my twenties.'

'Of course.' Felipe smiled, eager to give her a personal tour of the Castillo Estate Winery. 'There are tastings and wine tours and, thanks to Thiago's vision and hard work, a brand-new restaurant with a world-class chef.'

'Sounds amazing,' she said, licking her lips in a distracting way that, despite his best intentions, made him desperate for a taste of that lovely mouth.

All night he'd secretly toyed with the idea of how to say goodnight. A cheek kiss, as was standard among Argentinians, seemed too impersonal, but if he brushed her lips with his, he might not be able to stop himself taking it further. Perhaps it was best to let Emilia dictate their goodbye.

'So Thiago is the brother who's getting married?' she asked.

'That's right. He's ten years younger than me,' Felipe said, grasping the topic of conversation to distract himself from how badly he wanted to kiss her—right there and then—but couldn't. 'Fortunately for me,' he continued, 'Thiago wanted to work for the family business when my parents retired.'

Why had he suggested a platonic date when they'd admitted they were attracted to each other? Yes, he'd friend zoned her and wanted her to feel comfortable after her first date failure, but enjoying her sparkling company knowing he couldn't take it further was like a form of self-inflicted torture...

'You didn't?' she asked with a curious frown, twirling the stem of her wineglass as she watched him thoughtfully.

She seemed genuinely interested in his personal life and the feeling was mutual. They'd been at the restaurant for almost two hours and hadn't once talked about work.

Felipe shook his head, the old familiar rumble of guilt lodging under his ribs like a stitch.

'At the time, when I told my parents I wanted to go to medical school at UBA,' he said, glancing down at the table, 'that caused quite the upset, as you can imagine. I think my parents dreamed of both their sons running the family business together, but I was drawn to the big city lights and to medicine. I'm not sure they've ever quite forgiven me.'

He grinned, his light-hearted tone hiding how his career choice still felt like a bone of contention between him and his family. Felipe had always felt protective of Thiago, and the pursuit of his surgical career had inadvertently placed a responsibility for the family business on his younger brother's shoulders, especially as their parents grew older.

The consequences of Felipe's decision had also spilled into his private life. He'd felt compelled to make his career a success, almost to prove to his family that he'd made the right choice. And while he'd worked long hours to build up his professional reputation in Buenos Aires, he'd unwittingly neglected his marriage.

'I'm sure they're proud of you both,' Emilia said, her stare moving over his face as if she was figuring him out and somehow knew that, for him, this was a touchy subject. 'How often do you get home for a visit?'

'Not as often as I'd like,' he admitted. 'You know how demanding our work can be, but Thiago and Violetta's wedding will be a chance to catch up with all my family in one hit. Every cloud has a silver lining and all that...'

Emilia eyed him intently. 'You're really dreading the wedding, aren't you?'

Felipe added fearless and intuitive to her growing list of positive attributes.

'Not the wedding itself...' He shrugged, sitting forward to rest his forearms on the table. 'Just the look of disappointment in my mother's eyes. She's desperate to be an *abuela*, and I'm afraid I've failed her miserably.'

He smiled, his regret that he wasn't a father only momentary. He had a great life—a comfortable home, a full social life and a challenging job he loved.

'But at least Thiago has time to redeem himself and produce a grandchild,' he added. 'His wife-to-be is younger than him and has already told him she wants at least two children, so it seems my mother will get her heart's desire after all.'

His smile widened with mischief. 'And I'll get to be cool uncle Felipe who spoils them with sweets and inappropriately expensive gifts.'

Emilia's tinkling laughter eased the restless

ache in his chest that came when he thought about Thiago, the wedding and his family's expectations.

After dinner, they headed outside. The restaurant opened onto the buzzing Plaza de Luco, a favourite gathering place for Argentinians keen to enjoy the abundant nightlife on offer. It was a balmy autumn evening with lots of people out and about, frequenting the city's many restaurants, cocktail bars and dance clubs.

'So, what did you think of your second date in twenty years?' Felipe asked, casually strolling at her side across the square. 'Please tell me it went better than the date with Mr Horny.' He'd definitely made Emilia relax and smile tonight, and hopefully negated her bad experience with that other guy.

'A hundred times better.' She laughed, her stare sweeping over him from head to toe. He walked a little taller. 'Tonight's date lasted two hours instead of twenty minutes, for one,' she said, stepping a little closer.

'Good food and wine are worth savouring,' he said, desperate to take her hand or offer her his arm, but he held back. He didn't want to make any moves on her, given how he'd promised they could be just friends.

'Secondly,' she added, 'you've asked me plenty

of personal questions and seemed genuinely interested in me.'

'I *am* genuinely interested,' he said, trying not to appear too smug that he'd bested Mr Horny.

'And thirdly,' she concluded, her twinkling gaze full of playfulness, 'you didn't once stare at my chest.'

Felipe kept his expression neutral as he nodded. Oh, he'd looked all right. He'd simply been subtle about it.

'But seriously, thanks for suggesting tonight.' She smiled up at him, her eyes sparkling. 'You have no idea how much you've set my mind at ease.'

'You're welcome,' he said, glad he could restore her faith in men. 'Take it from your dating coach—a date shouldn't feel like a trip to the dentist.'

'Well, you're the expert,' she said with a curious expression on her face. 'Fifteen years is a long time to date without falling into a serious relationship.'

'I guess,' he said with another shrug, because he'd never before considered how his lifestyle choices might appear from the outside. 'What can I say—I enjoy the company of beautiful, intelligent women.'

And until Emilia had walked into his life, he'd never once questioned his behaviour. Dating was a means to an end. He enjoyed socialising and eating out and had a healthy sex drive. But now that he'd met her, he realised how many of his other dates had been empty somehow, although it was his choice to keep things superficial. There was something special about her that left him unsettled, as if he knew he could be happier. But perhaps it was just this inconvenient attraction to her that he had to constantly battle.

'Plus, what's a single person too young to be all alone supposed to do?' he asked, playfully. 'I'm always safe and responsible, and I think I show my dates a good time. I've certainly never had any complaints.'

'I should hope so.' She laughed, stepping aside as they passed a large group of people—her arm brushed his.

Felipe reflexively offered her his arm, and to his relief, she accepted, sliding her hand through his elbow. He hid his body's shudder of excitement.

'At least now you have some tips and pointers for the next time you go on a date, and can easily dismiss anyone who doesn't make the grade.' Hopefully, he'd set the bar nice and high. Except the idea of her dating other men only intensified that restlessness in him.

He wanted to take her out again, but it was complicated. As she'd pointed out they worked together. He'd have to provide a report on her for the Argentine Medical Council. She was still grieving, vulnerable and he genuinely wanted to be her friend.

'Shall we take a taxi,' he asked, as they arrived at the taxi rank. 'If you don't mind, I'd like to see you home? No strings, I promise. I'm just a bit old fashioned like that.'

Emilia looked up at him, an enigmatic look in her eyes that gave nothing away. 'Isn't it out of your way?'

Her teeth dragged at her distracting bottom lip as if she was waiting, thinking, maybe even plotting. Felipe couldn't stop staring, still arguing back and forth with himself if he should kiss her goodnight. Would their chemistry be as hot as he imagined, or would a harmless kiss ruin their budding friendship?

'It's worth it for a little longer in your company, if you don't mind,' he said, holding up his hands in supplication. 'But it's totally your call.'

She hesitated, wrapping her arms around her waist as if she was cold. Felipe shrugged off his sports jacket and draped it over her shoulders.

She smiled up at him. 'Thank you.' She blinked, something conflicted shifting behind her eyes. 'I'd like your company for a little longer too, but I have a nosy teenager at my place.' She stepped closer, vulnerability in her eyes that told Felipe how uncertain and out of practice she was when it came to interacting with men. 'You could, um… invite me back to your place for a nightcap?'

Felipe froze, his heart racing with excitement, but his head applied the brakes. Just because she wasn't ready for their evening to end just yet— and the feeling was definitely mutual—didn't mean she wanted more than just his company. If anything more was ever to happen between them, he would need very clear signals from her. Except it was taking all his strength to resist the temptation to kiss her. Having her in his apartment would test him further, but more than anything he wanted her to be comfortable with him, his protective urges flaring to life.

'I'd love that,' he said, 'but I only live a five-minute walk from here and it's a beautiful night. Shall we walk?'

Emilia nodded, seeming to relax. They set off at a leisurely pace, side by side. This time she spontaneously looped her warm hand around his arm, her touch electrifying his skin through the thin cotton of his shirt, as her perfume wafted on the cool evening air.

Just like that his restless feeling evaporated.

But he needed to be so careful with this woman. Unlike the strangers he often dated while also keeping at arms' length, there was so much more at stake: their working relationship, their budding friendship, Emilia settling into an unfamiliar city where she had no other friends. They couldn't allow lust to cloud their judgement, and Emilia was new to casual dating. He didn't want to hurt her somehow or inadvertently let her down after everything she'd been through.

'So, tell me about your husband,' he asked after a moment's silence, the subject a timely reminder of another obstacle he needed to be mindful of. 'What kind of lawyer was he?'

Emilia glanced up at him as if surprised by his interest. 'He specialised in commercial law,' she said, a small half-smile on her lips. 'He and a friend from university started their own firm in Montevideo. He was very successful.'

Felipe nodded encouragingly and she continued.

'Then, at only forty-seven,' she said, 'he was diagnosed with glioblastoma multiforme.'

Felipe winced, regretting that he'd made her feel sad. GBM was the most aggressive form of brain cancer.

'I'm sorry. That must have been hard on all of you. What a tragic waste.' He squeezed her hand between his elbow and his side, letting her know that he understood her grief, which was so evident in her beautiful eyes.

She shrugged but then swallowed, as if with effort. 'Within two years, he was dead. Eva was only thirteen, a real Papá's girl, so of course, it hit her the hardest.'

Her voice fell. She ducked her head and Felipe wished he'd chosen a lighter topic of conversation. But a part of him wanted to know everything about her, even this.

'And you lost the love of your life,' he pointed out. 'It's hard on both you *and* Eva.'

As a solo parent, she was probably used to putting her needs last, but her grief was every bit as valid as Eva's.

'Yes,' she admitted, watching him for a few seconds. 'But I just got on with things. I had a teenager to raise, so I couldn't afford to break down. I didn't want Eva's young life to be derailed by my grief. Besides, wallowing wouldn't have brought Ricardo back.'

Felipe rested his hand over hers on his arm. 'That's understandable. You felt you had to set aside your own grieving process to focus on Eva. It's not surprising that dating has been a low priority for you until now.'

She nodded, her eyes alight with what looked like gratitude. 'Thanks for asking about Ricardo. It means a lot to me. Many people are scared to ask about him in case I find the reminder too upsetting, but that means it can sometimes feel as if there's no one I can talk to about him.'

'You're welcome, Emilia. Any time you need

to talk, I'm here.' Out of nowhere, a fresh surge of protectiveness built inside him.

She was amazing. She had a busy and emotionally demanding career, she'd raised her daughter alone for the past five years, while also grieving, and now she'd moved to a new country.

'This is my building,' he said, pausing in front of a modern apartment block facing the park in Palermo, a fashionable central city district. 'Dante and I are in the penthouse.'

She smiled, flashing her dimple. 'Of course you are.' But her teasing seemed to break the tension.

'Hey, it has the best views,' he said, scanning the building's electronic lock with his key fob.

'Another of your dating moves?' she asked, pushing inside to the building's foyer. 'Wow women with your penthouse apartment?'

Felipe reached for her hand and tugged her towards the lift. 'That's rookie dating mistake number one.' He winked, enjoying the laughter in her eyes. 'Never invite a first date back to your place. If she turns out to be too clingy, then there's no escape—she knows exactly where you live.'

Emilia shook her head as if in wonder. 'Oh, well done you. But see, I didn't even think of that. I have so much to learn.' She stepped inside the lift at his side.

Felipe gently squeezed her hand and pressed the

button for the top floor. 'Well, that's why we're here. This is a practice date, remember?'

Only right then, he was struggling to think about anything but how much he wished it was the real thing.

CHAPTER SEVEN

As Felipe retook his seat in the living room, after taking Dante out for a quick toilet break and then settling him in the spare bedroom, Emilia sipped her brandy, the warmth sliding through her stomach and infecting her limbs like a much-needed dose of liquid courage.

He smelled so good… She could hardly believe that she'd boldly suggested coming back to his place, but his charming, unthreatening company was so easy to enjoy. Tonight he'd made her feel safe and attractive. Light-hearted. He'd been funny and attentive and considerate, his assurances that they could just be friends completely removing the pressure from the situation. He'd even asked about Ricardo, giving her the space to talk about her husband beyond the illness that had stolen him from her.

She hadn't wanted the evening to end and couldn't have asked for more from a first date.

Only this was a *fake* date. A practice run. And

unlike Emilia, committed bachelor Felipe was the expert at dating.

'So,' she said, gulping another sip of brandy to abolish her regrets that she'd been so brave to suggest this nightcap, 'your ex-wife got the house and you ended up here?' A stunning penthouse apartment in central Buenos Aires. She glanced around, appreciatively, finding the space modern, minimalist and very masculine. The spectacular city views alone would most definitely wow any single woman who set foot in the place. And with fifteen years of casual dating, there must surely have been many women to impress.

Jealousy, hot and shocking, slid through her veins. But she didn't want to think about Felipe's *other* dating moves, the ones that led to tangled, sweaty sheets and very satisfied women...

This close to him, lured by the romance of his views, and with his earlier talk of a healthy sex life fresh in her mind, she was already struggling to think about anything else beyond how much she wanted to kiss him. But the staggering strength of her attraction aside, was she ready for such a momentous step?

He shrugged, his eyes steady on hers as they had been all evening. 'I offered Delfina the house, but in the end we split everything fifty-fifty and each moved on. Only fair. I didn't want to squabble over *that's mine, this is yours* and there were no children to consider.'

Emilia watched him in rapt fascination. She liked the respectful way he spoke about his ex-wife, with courtesy and mild indifference. It was obvious he had no lingering feelings, not that it was any of *her* business.

'So where is she now, your ex?' she asked, her inhibitions lowered by the way he'd made her feel—as if her body and desires were coming back to life. He seemed like such a catch, such a gentleman and a good listener. She couldn't imagine what might have gone wrong in his marriage.

Felipe glanced out at the lights of Buenos Aires below. 'She lives on the other side of the city, although we hardly ever see each other. I wish her well. We were married for fifteen years, and I played my part in the demise of our relationship.'

'Did you cheat?' she asked, intrigued. She couldn't imagine him being unfaithful. He was too honest.

'No, but I spent a lot of time at work.' He turned back to face her, his stare bold and steady, as if he owned his mistakes. 'I can't blame my ex for making a separate life for herself.'

'Did *she* cheat?' Emilia realised the moment the question was out that she was being nosy. But she was too relaxed, too focused on the self-generated heat of attraction making her languid. And what kind of woman would let Felipe escape?

His lip curled as he placed his glass on the table. 'Not as far as I know. But we woke up one day and had nothing to talk about. I think we both realised there should be more passion, more fire to a relationship than that, even after all those years together.'

Emilia nodded, aware that she and Ricardo had had their challenges in their marriage too, but had loved each other passionately to the end, maybe because they'd also been best friends.

'So, what brought you two together in the first place?' She was pushing, but she wanted to know what kind of a man he was outside of work, where he was a dedicated, well-respected surgeon. He'd mentioned letting his family down over his choice of career, but what intense passions, what fire had driven a younger Felipe?

'Sex.' He grinned as he stared intently into her eyes.

Emilia's body went up in flames and she dragged in a shuddering breath. Was everything about sex tonight?

Felipe turned serious. 'We also shared drive and ambition, and a desire to leave our small town for the thrill of Buenos Aires. But when passion cools, and if that drive takes you in different directions, you suddenly realise that you're married to someone with whom you have little in common.'

'I'm sorry it didn't work out for you,' Emilia said, sensing his regret. A high-achieving man like Felipe would likely baulk at any form of failure. 'What does Delfina do?'

Talking about his ex-wife was helping her to rationalise her own body's reaction to him. It was understandable that after so many years of grief and loneliness her physical desires would eventually reawaken. Especially as she felt safe with Felipe. Respected.

'She works in fashion,' he said. 'She's a buyer for the fashion brand Hermoso.'

His stare moved over her face as it had several times tonight. Was he wondering if he should kiss her? Was that usually the way his dates ended?

'That explains why you're always so stylishly dressed,' she said, the last word emerging a little strangled as lust swept through her at the idea of kissing Felipe Castillo.

But was she seriously considering it after only kissing one man for so long? Imagining the previously unimaginable, her heart thumped and her mind went crazy with questions.

Would it be as exciting as she imagined, life-affirming? Or would it leave her riddled with embarrassment, regret and guilt? Would kissing Felipe be a betrayal of her beloved Ricardo, of his memory and everything they'd shared during their marriage? Or was she overthinking it, terrified by how badly she wanted to find out the answers?

As if aware of the direction of her thoughts, Felipe stilled. 'I think you look beautiful in that dress,' he said in a tight voice. 'That's a great colour on you. Makes your beautiful eyes shine.'

Emilia swallowed hard, blinked at the intensity of his eye contact. Stunned by the honesty of his compliment.

He thought she was beautiful. She dragged in a breath, tired of her mind's back and forth. Tired of fighting the demands of her body. Tired of having this fear of being intimate with anyone else hanging over her like a storm cloud. Sometimes you just needed to take a chance and try new things.

'I don't know if it's the brandy,' she said in a whisper, her heartrate flying, 'or maybe your apartment's spectacular views, but I really want to kiss you.'

The air left her in a rush, as if she'd jumped from a plane but her parachute had opened. There was a second's pause that felt like an hour where he simply stared at her, immobile. Had she judged it wrong? Was it a terrible idea given they were colleagues? But surely no one else needed to know—

'Thanks goodness for that,' he said, exhaling

harshly and glancing down at her lips with hungry eyes. 'I was starting to get desperate over here. I've wanted to kiss you all evening.'

Without hesitation and before she could second guess her impulse, he cupped her face between his palms, then slowly and deliberately leaned in and brushed her lips with his. A soft teasing swipe that tasted of brandy, and elicited a low sigh in the back of his throat.

Her lips tingled, her adrenaline spiking. Long-forgotten need roared to life, hijacking her body and obliterating her thoughts.

She blinked, dragged in a shuddering breath for courage as she looked up at him. She hadn't done this in so long, but as thrilling and tantalising as that whisper of a kiss was, she didn't want it to end. It had been alien but wonderful and far too brief.

As she sensed him pulling back, she raised one hand to his cheek. She sighed as their lips met again. This time, Felipe lingered, his lips softly gliding over hers again and again as if slowly and thoroughly learning their shape and savouring their taste.

Despite the frantic galloping of her heart, Emilia relaxed into it. Felipe was obviously taking it slow, giving her time to adjust, a chance to dictate the pace or maybe to apply the brakes. Her eyes stung with emotion. He was so thoughtful. He must have guessed that a huge part of her, the part that still felt married to Ricardo, was crushed with guilt for kissing another man. But Ricardo was gone, and ignoring the physical demands of her body, staying faithful to his memory, wouldn't bring him back.

Because she wanted a night off from feeling sad and alone. Emilia closed her eyes and allowed herself to enjoy kissing Felipe. As if it was natural, she parted her lips, tentatively touching her tongue to Felipe's. Her body melted as his arm came around her waist and his lips turned more insistent, commanding their kiss, the passion building until it was all she could do to forget about breathing for a while, clinging to his toned body and strong arms and kissing him back.

Disorienting forces tugged her in opposing directions. This felt both wrong and wonderfully right. But if she had to get over this intimacy hurdle with anyone, she'd much rather it be mature, considerate Felipe than some unpredictable stranger she'd met on a dating app.

At last, Felipe pulled back, his breathing harsh. 'I have a confession to make.' He pushed her hair back from her warm face, his stare flitting over her as if checking she was okay.

She nodded for him to continue, her lips desperate for more.

'I *did* look at your chest earlier.' A sexy flash

of excitement lit his eyes. 'I just did it discreetly.' His gaze swept lower now, to her lips, her cleavage and back. Emilia felt scorched, restless, needy. 'You have a great body,' he said, resting his hands on her shoulders, his thumbs swiping back and forth over her bare skin.

She swallowed, thrilled and electrified by his simple touch. 'So do you.'

He was so sexy. And nice and decent and dedicated. She instinctively knew she could trust him. Kissing him didn't have to be a big deal.

With a shaking hand, she placed her glass aside and reached for his waist, leaning into him and kissing him again. She wanted the liberating pleasure of their undeniable chemistry.

The second kiss was even better, as if they'd learned the shape of the other person and everything instantly and effortlessly slotted exactly where it should. Only now that it was more familiar, it was also more intense.

His fingers slid into her hair, urging her closer. She gripped his shirt at the waist, her lips and tongue bolder against his. He slanted his mouth over hers, deepening their kiss, and she moaned, the sound forced from her throat by the euphoric excitement of being kissed properly again—with heat. Being this in sync with another person. Being desired.

Maybe she could let go of her doubts and reservations and embrace her desire for this man. Neither of them was looking for anything serious, and they were mature enough to stop their personal lives bleeding into their professional relationship.

Heat pooled in her pelvis as the embrace turned more passionate. He hauled her close, his strong arms banded around her waist so her breasts grazed his chest as their tongues surged together. In an instant, she was too hot. Achy. She couldn't seem to get close enough to Felipe. She wanted more.

'You are so incredibly sexy,' he groaned, shifting back against the sofa and tugging her with him, pressing kisses to her jaw and neck. 'I'm so glad you moved to Buenos Aires.'

Emilia smiled as she sat astride his lap, holding his face between her palms. 'That's very flattering.'

'Do you realise how rare this is, just clicking with someone so effortlessly?' He smiled softly, cupping her face tenderly as if he understood how she must be feeling—both exhilarated and guilt-ridden.

'Is it?' she asked, knowing he was right. She had a sneaking suspicion that she'd have to date a lot of guys to find one as perfect for her on paper as Felipe.

But this was about physical desire, nothing more. To remind herself of that, she leaned in and kissed him again. She wanted to feel, not to think. She wanted to set everything else aside and focus on *her* needs for once. To admit that while she would always love her husband she was human. A woman. A sexual being.

Distracting her from the sudden spike of fear, his hands gripped her hips, and he crushed her close. He was hard, his stare dark with arousal as he looked up at her, letting her dictate the pace of whatever this was. Both scared and desperate, Emilia shifted on his lap so their bodies aligned, the steel of him and the heat of her as she pressed kisses down the side of his neck.

This felt too good to stop. It was as if he'd awoken every cell in her body and they urgently wanted the same thing.

'I want you,' she whispered, pulling back to look at him. Her pulse buzzed in her ears, but it felt right. Felipe wasn't some stranger. He'd shown her the kind of man he was these past few days. She felt safe with him, safe to explore the ferocious arousal he'd inspired in her.

'Are you sure?' He watched her face, his hands guiding her hips into a hypnotic rhythm that seemed to appease them both.

But the friction wasn't enough. After so many years of denying her sexuality, need built inside Emilia like a tornado.

'I'm certain.' She nodded, her fingers undoing the top few buttons of his shirt, exposing his bronzed chest that was dusted with manly dark hair. 'Only it's been so long for me,' she said, a second of doubt gripping her like a cold fist.

What if she'd forgotten the moves? She'd loved one man most of her adult life. Her hesitance to be intimate with someone new made sense. But now wasn't the time to think about her husband.

'I know…' Felipe groaned, his hands fisting the fabric of her dress at her hips, as if he was holding back. 'That's why I want you to be sure.'

Emilia nodded, panic squeezing her lungs. What if it was horrible and they ruined their working relationship and their friendship? What if she chickened out and missed this chance? 'I am sure, if you are. Just tonight.'

She was a mature woman who knew what she wanted. With Felipe, she felt seen and understood and respected. That was enough for her.

'Deal—then we go back to being friends.' His eyes darkened with arousal. 'I wanted you the first time I saw you,' he said, his hands moving slowly from her hips to cup her breasts. 'I know, very inappropriate at work…and me your supervisor…'

Emilia gasped as his thumbs rubbed over her nipples through her dress, sending dizzying waves of pleasure through her entire body. 'Don't forget dating coach,' she said with a smile, before leaning in to kiss him again.

He was right. A connection like theirs was rare, made all the more perfect by the fact that they wanted the same things—no strings. Just one night of passion.

His hands caressed her breasts, the delicious friction dragging a moan from her throat. 'Felipe...' She dropped her head back and closed her eyes, awash with sensation. She was going to do this. Sleep with a sexy work colleague and have no regrets.

'I want to make you feel good,' he said, while Emilia leaned over him, lost in kissing his chest, the side of his neck and the angle of his jaw. His warm hands skimmed along the length of her thighs, raising the hem of her silky dress over her hips.

'Me too,' she said, too far gone to hesitate as she lifted her arms overhead so he could quickly remove the garment.

He tossed it aside, his stare feasting on her near naked body with thrilling hunger. His hands followed the path of his stare, gliding over her hips, her waist and her breasts.

Watching his hands on her skin, Emilia bit down on her bottom lip, trying to contain the firestorm of need coursing through her veins. She couldn't wait any longer—she'd waited long enough. Overcome with urgency, Emilia popped the remaining buttons on his shirt and hurriedly tackled his trouser fly, her fingers clumsy in their haste.

As if reluctant to simply be undressed, Felipe dragged her mouth back to his and expertly unclasped her bra with a single pinch. As he removed it, his mouth sought out one nipple and then the other. She shuddered against him as if she'd never before been touched.

He groaned, sucking her nipple until she gasped and her head swam. She ached from head to toe, her heart banging wildly and fire scorching her every nerve.

'Yes…' she moaned, sliding her fingers through his thick hair and watching his mouth on her breast.

Breaking free, Felipe threw off his shirt and trousers and laid her back against the cool leather of his sofa. His gorgeous, toned body covered hers so she was engulfed by heat and steel and flexing power. It was so good to feel desired again, to feel that neglected part of herself—her sexuality—unfurl and come back to vibrant life.

His tongue dipped inside her mouth, his hips grinding against hers so they groaned in unison, the wildness building. Emilia shoved at his boxers, cupping his erection. He thrust his tongue against hers with a throaty growl, and the urgency ramped up a notch. There was a frantic scramble while they removed their underwear and he reached for a condom from his wallet.

Gripping Felipe's shoulders as he rolled on the condom, she pulled him down on top of her, kissing him deeply. She was burning up, awash with arousal, desperate for the release building inside. Felipe's hand slid between her legs, his fingers stroking her so there was no room in her head for anything but pleasure and passion. As he touched her, he pulled back from their kiss to peer down at her, need stark in the set of his jaw and the depths of his dark eyes.

'I want you,' Emilia said again, because she didn't want there to be any doubt in his mind.

She spread her thighs and hooked her legs around his hips, drawing him closer. He reared back, braced on his arms, and with their stares locked he pushed inside her, watching her gasp with pleasure. Triumph and excitement darkened his eyes to almost black.

Emilia gripped his face, bringing his mouth back to her kiss. He was such a good kisser. She couldn't seem to get enough. He moved inside her, his fingers teasing her nipples and his tongue thrusting against hers so every part of her felt electrified, alive. Emilia slid her hands over the taut muscles and smooth skin of his shoulders, his back, his buttocks, her senses flooded with the scent and feel of him and the sound of his sexy groans.

Her orgasm built swift and strong. She cried out his name and he reared back, watching her disintegrate, his thrusts speeding up so sweat slicked his bronzed skin. With a hoarse shout he came, burying his face against the side of her neck, clutching her so tightly through the body-racking spasms she almost couldn't breathe.

But who cared about breathing after sex that good?

Emilia lay still as he slipped from her body, her heart still racing against his.

'That was amazing,' she said, initially feeling a massive weight off her shoulders. Just what she'd needed to get her confidence back. But now that it was over, awkwardness rushed in, smothering down all the lovely endorphins.

Her mind unhelpfully produced fresh doubts. What was the one-night stand protocol? Should she dress and leave straight away? Thank him and say, *'See you Monday'*?

'It was.' Felipe stirred, raising his face from the side of her neck and looking down at her with a soft, slightly dazed smile. He brushed the hair back from her face and pressed languid kisses to her lips. 'How do you feel?' he asked, sliding to the side but keeping his hand on her waist.

His question was so unexpected that her eyes

started to sting with the release of pent-up emotion. Silly—it was only sex. But for so many years, sex for Emilia had been about love.

'Good,' she said, her hand stroking up and down his strong arm, from elbow to shoulder, as if seeking comfort. 'How about you?'

His smile widened. 'I feel fantastic. So, no regrets?' he pressed, his intent gaze moving over her face as if he really cared that she was okay with her decision to sleep with him.

'Not one.'

'I'm glad.' He pressed one final kiss to her lips, then reached for a tissue from the end table and dealt with the condom. Then he stood and took her hand, pulling her to her feet.

For a few seconds they stood naked, facing each other with goofy smiles on their faces. Then he slid his stare down her naked body and started to get hard again.

'Wanna see my bedroom?' he asked with a sexy flick of his brows, letting her know he was up for round two if she was. 'The views are even better.'

Emilia laughed, nodded, her breath snatched away by excitement. 'Yes, but then I have to get home. Parental curfew.'

He reached for her hand and led the way. 'I don't want to get you into trouble.'

Emilia stood on tiptoes and pressed her body and mouth to his. 'Then stop talking.'

CHAPTER EIGHT

EARLY MONDAY MORNING, Felipe strode onto the NICU to find Emilia already at Luis Lopez's bedside with both her registrar and his. They'd agreed to review the baby's post-op progress together, but now that the moment had come to face her and act as if Friday night hadn't happened, he felt an uncharacteristic shudder of apprehension.

'Dr Gonzales,' he said, his stare meeting hers across their tiny patient while his heart banged with excitement. She looked beautiful as usual, only now he knew exactly how every part of her body looked and felt and tasted.

'Good morning, Dr Castillo,' she replied, her expression neutral, giving nothing away.

Was it just his imagination, or did she seem a little subdued this morning? Friday night, she'd reassured him that she had no regrets, but maybe with the whole weekend to ponder what they'd done she'd changed her mind. He'd considered calling her over the weekend to make sure she was okay, but she'd been on call at the hospital, and they'd agreed to put that one night behind them.

Not that he could blame her if she did feel derailed. The events of Friday night had certainly taken him aback. They'd had a great date, they'd opened up to each other about their pasts, and as for the sex... He hadn't expected their easy connection to turn so heated, nor had he anticipated how much he'd want to see her again outside of work, like for that walk in the dog park perhaps...

Deciding it was best that he *hadn't* succumbed to the impulse to call her, Felipe turned to his registrar, Dr Ruiz. He listened to the latest blood results on Luis, while simultaneously trying to come to terms with that insanely hot night with his new colleague.

Now that they'd slept together, his awareness of her was finely tuned—the subtle scent of her perfume, the length of her dark eyelashes, the visible softness of those lovely full lips. Only he needed to put the amazing sex into perspective and act normally. He didn't want any awkwardness to ruin their friendship and, as her supervisor, he needed to show discretion at work.

'Luis has had multiple apnoeic spells this morning,' his registrar said, thankfully oblivious to the tension between Felipe and Emilia.

Felipe nodded, gently pressing his stethoscope against the baby's tiny chest, listening to the rapid beat of his heart and the whoosh of air in and out of his lungs.

'Chest is clear. Heart sounds normal,' he said, glancing at Emilia for her input.

Apnoea, when breathing stopped for a significant period of time, was common in pre-term infants, but Luis Lopez was only three days post-op. His left lung was still small and underdeveloped because of the diaphragmatic hernia. The last thing they needed was for his recovery to be hampered by a chest infection or some other post operative complication. He watched as Emilia gently palpated Luis's abdomen.

'It's soft,' she said. 'No evidence of peritonitis or a collection and the wound looks good.' Their eyes met as they each pondered the likely cause of Luis's apnoea.

Felipe's heart rate spiked with excitement and uncertainty. He wished he knew how she felt after their date. He didn't want that night to ruin the easy working relationship they'd developed, and he still valued her friendship.

'We could repeat the scan to make sure the internal repair is sound,' Felipe suggested, concerned for the smallest Lopez triplet. 'The chest drain is patent, so it's unlikely to be a haemothorax.' Only they didn't want to miss something.

'Surgically everything seems stable,' Emilia agreed, and then turned to face her registrar.

'Have we run a blood glucose recently? Hypo-glycaemia can cause central apnoea.'

Very low birth weight babies often suffered low blood sugar, especially when feeding was interrupted by surgery, as in Luis's case. One registrar made a note in Luis's file, while the other organised the blood work.

'While we're checking that,' Felipe said to them, 'let's retest electrolytes and blood gases too.'

'Are you happy to recommence nasogastric feeds?' Emilia asked him as the neonatal nurse switched out the intravenous saline for glucose. 'Feeding will help stabilise blood sugars.'

'Sounds good,' he said, glancing back down at Luis. 'Let's leave our team to sort all that while we speak to Isabella and Sebastian.'

Together, they found the couple in the family room and explained Luis's progress to them.

'From a surgical standpoint,' Felipe told the Lopezes, 'everything looks good. There's no sign of complications, but we're concerned that his blood sugars might be a little low. We'll test for that, and re-establish the nasogastric tube feeding regime today and wean Luis off the oxygen. Keep bringing in your expressed breast milk.'

Isabella nodded and glanced at Emilia, as if for her confirmation. But of course, the women had met before the babies were born, and mother-to-mother, they shared a bond.

'The surgery went very smoothly,' Emilia confirmed, looking to Felipe to include him in the conversation. 'But to be on the safe side, Dr Castillo's registrar is going to order some blood tests and repeat the scan.'

After a few more questions, the couple seemed relieved and headed back to the NICU, hand in hand.

'Can we talk for a second?' Felipe asked Emilia as they left the third floor and took the stairs down to Theatres.

'Of course,' Emilia said, glancing his way as they entered the surgical department. 'Is everything okay?' Doubt flickered across her eyes, and Felipe offered her a reassuring nod.

'Of course.' He indicated his office and followed her inside, closing the door behind them.

She turned to face him with an expectant smile. Felipe hesitated. Perhaps he'd misjudged her withdrawal. Perhaps she'd put Friday night well behind her and was simply getting her head into another working week after the weekend. Perhaps it was only *him* who'd been rocked to the core by what had happened.

'I just wanted to make sure you were okay after Friday night?' he said, diving straight in to dispense with any awkwardness. 'You were gone when I woke up. Sorry that I fell asleep. Not very gentlemanly of me…'

Emilia shook her head, a delicate flush on her cheeks as she reached for his arm and gave it a reassuring squeeze. 'It's no problem. I had to sneak home before Eva realised I wasn't back. I felt like a teenager again, creeping into my own house.'

She grinned and Felipe's doubts settled, his entire body relaxing for the first time since he'd walked onto the NICU earlier. She was a capable, mature woman who knew what she wanted. There was obviously no awkwardness between them this morning. But a niggle of unease lingered. Was he disappointed to return to just being friends?

'You called a taxi?' he asked, a part of him wishing she hadn't needed to rush off. He usually tried to avoid having women sleeping over in favour of keeping things casual, but she'd felt far too good in his arms, warming his bed.

She shrugged. 'I didn't want to wake you.'

The second time, after a shared shower, they'd taken things slower. In his king-sized bed, he'd kissed every part of her body, bringing her to climax with his mouth before pushing inside her once more.

She dropped her hand to her side, and he quickly snagged hold of her fingers.

'So we're good?' he pressed, peering into her eyes. 'No awkward feelings? No regrets?'

Why was he so invested in making sure she'd had a good time? And why was he still dazed by how hot they'd been together? Emilia was a passionate, experienced woman.

Her smile softened and she inched closer, keeping her fingers entwined with his. 'I had a lovely night, Felipe, although it went a bit further than I expected for a first date...'

'Then it's a good thing it wasn't a *real* date,' he said with a smile, 'just a practice run.'

She laughed and the sound lifted his spirits, any reservations he had about them sleeping together and working together dissolving. But, despite thinking they were done, that everything would return to their pre-sex vibe, he found himself desperate to kiss her again, if only to make sure it was as good in the cold light of day. Not that he truly needed the experiment. Their chemistry was as strong as ever, which was maybe the main reason he *shouldn't* kiss her again. They'd promised each other—just one night.

'I wanted to thank you, actually,' she said, a little hesitantly, looking up at him. 'You can imagine how apprehensive I was to be intimate with anyone else. No matter how illogical it might be, part of me still felt guilty, as if I was...cheating.'

Empathy gripped him. 'I can understand that,' he said, a lump in his throat that she felt comfortable enough to confess such a personal detail.

'But you were so considerate and thoughtful,' she added, squeezing his fingers. '*Definitely* a gentleman.'

She stepped closer, looking up at him with that open expression, and his body instantly reacted, desire and protective urges flaring, every muscle tensing, his temperature shooting through the roof. He still wanted her, just as much as before. Only they'd agreed to one night. His head should be on their working relationship, not sex…

Only with Emilia, it was more than just great sex. They were friends, too.

'I had a really good time,' she went on, sincerely. 'I want you to know that, thanks to you, I feel as if a weight has been lifted from my shoulders, somehow.' She closed the distance between them and raised her face to his, pressing a swift kiss beside his mouth.

Felipe froze, his first instinct to forget their working relationship, forget friendship, to spear his fingers through her hair, crush her body to his and drag her mouth back to his. It was a natural urge after their red-hot night. But Emilia was different to the other women he'd dated, and he needed to stay professional.

'You're welcome,' he said, his stare snagged on her parted lips and the soft gust of her rapid breaths. 'I had a really good time, too.' The best time he'd had in years. Maybe that was why he had an uncharacteristic urge to see her again.

For a handful of seconds, they stared at each other, smiling, as if suspended in time. Emotions flitted across her face: excitement, hesitation, that telling flicker of desire.

Felipe snapped. To hell with their working relationship. He'd been denied that goodbye kiss when she'd left his bed in the early hours of Saturday morning. It would be almost rude not to take the opportunity to do it now.

Done wrestling with his thoughts, and because she was still holding his hand, he scooped one arm around her waist, cupped her cheek with his other hand, hauled her close and kissed her. Emilia met him halfway, surging up on her tiptoes to cement their kiss.

As if they'd both been holding back, the first touch of lips to lips unleashed a torrent of arousal. She moaned—he released a low growl in the back of his throat. How was he expected to resist this amazing woman who was now a friend, a colleague, a passionate lover?

Without breaking contact, he spun them around and pressed her back against the closed office door so he could align her body to his in all the places that mattered. She whimpered a sexy little sound that inflamed him further, her fingers tangling in his hair.

He pinned her to the door with his grinding hips, their bodies touching from shoulder to thigh, moving restlessly together as if to deepen the friction and seek out release. Her hands gripped his neck, keeping their lips locked together, their tongues surging, teasing, tasting. Drugged with desire, Felipe cupped her breast through her shirt, his thumb toying the nipple erect until she moaned and dropped her head back against the door.

'Felipe…' she gasped, staring up at him, her teeth snagging her bottom lip, which was swollen from their kisses.

'That's the goodbye kiss I would have given you if you'd woken me before you left,' he said, dragging his lips over her throat and sucking in the heady scent of her skin.

'Then I'm really sorry I missed it,' she panted, palming his erection through his trousers as she pulled his mouth back to hers.

He needed to stop this. They couldn't be caught making out in his office. They had a full morning of surgeries about to begin and they were supposed to be done with the physical side of their relationship.

Only his head and his body were in direct conflict.

Finally, with a strength he hadn't known he possessed, Felipe dragged his mouth from hers and let his hands slip to her waist. 'Sorry about that. I got carried away. I felt as if I'd been cheated out of that one last kiss by falling asleep.'

She smiled sheepishly, smoothing down her blouse. 'I'm sorry, too. You're very good at kissing.'

He smiled and they stepped away from each other, as if physical distance would squash further temptation. While Felipe dragged in some calming breaths, Emilia glanced at the door and sobered. 'That night was just between us, right? I wouldn't want anyone here to know.'

'Of course.' Felipe brushed a hand down his shirt and straightened his tie, shrugging off disappointment. While he was still reeling over how much he still wanted her, in spite of their promise to each other, she was more pragmatic. 'But do you really need to ask?'

She was right to reset the boundaries. They were professionals. He was her supervisor. And he respected her as a friend.

'No,' she said, shaking her head. 'Sorry. Perhaps I just needed to remind *myself* that we're at work. You're kind of irresistible.' Her stare flicked to his groin, where he was still tenting the front of his trousers. For an agonised second, he couldn't tell if she was about to kiss him again or leave.

Then she rested her hand on the doorknob at her back, her intentions clear. It was time to shelve their chemistry and put work first.

'I might need a second,' he said with a wince, stepping behind his desk to put a piece of heavy furniture between him and Emilia.

Shooting one last almost wistful glance below his belt, she nodded. 'I'll um…go and get changed. See you in Theatre.'

It took him a solid five minutes to calm down.

CHAPTER NINE

'I'M HOME,' Emilia called later that night, closing the front door behind her, kicking off her shoes and bending to give a welcoming Luna an ear-rub.

After a day with back-to-back surgeries, her feet were killing her. But the throbbing helped to keep her mind off Felipe and that incredibly reckless but raunchy kiss in his office. What had she been thinking? Anyone could have walked in and caught them getting steamy against the door, and they'd promised to return to being just friends. But she hadn't been able to help herself after their seriously sexy night together.

She'd spent the entire weekend with a dreamy smile on her face, reliving every steamy second. Their *date* had given her back her confidence. And today he'd been so thoughtful and considerate, checking that she'd had no regrets. She had no hope of resisting one more kiss. But it had taken all her strength to walk away. If they hadn't been at work, if they hadn't made it clear it was a one-off thing, she would have absolutely slept with him again. He was just so good in bed…

Fanning her face to cool down, she shrugged off her coat and tried to shove aside the memories. It was done. Time to move on. No more thinking about his sexy smile, or the way he touched her face, or that soft groan he made whenever he crushed her in his strong arms…

'I'm making dinner,' Eva called from the kitchen, sounding cheerfully upbeat.

Emilia joined Eva in the kitchen, pouring herself a glass of red wine, trying to appear like a fifty-two-year-old woman who hadn't had mind-blowing sex at the weekend.

And almost again at work today…

'Smells delicious,' she said, stirring the pot to distract herself from thinking about Felipe's skill as a lover. 'Thank you for cooking. My last surgery ran overtime.'

Eva batted her mother's hand away, so Emilia took a seat at the breakfast bar to sip her wine and watch dinner progressing.

'So how was your second date on Friday night?' Eva asked, hope shining in her big brown eyes. 'I didn't hear you come in and we've hardly seen each other since.'

Eva had played social volleyball on Saturday and spent most of Sunday at the law library, while

Emilia had been on call, spending much of the weekend at the hospital.

Emilia took another sip of wine and prayed that she wouldn't blush and give herself away. It should be *Eva* sneaking home in the early hours after a hot date, not the other way around.

'It was nice,' she said evasively, uncomfortable with why she hadn't told Eva about the non-date date before now. But a part of her hadn't wanted to answer questions about her and Felipe, and Eva had already considered him interested in Emilia.

'Better than the first one, I hope,' Eva pressed, shrewdly watching her mother for more details.

Emilia nodded. 'Yes. Although it wasn't a *real* date. Felipe, the guy you met that night at Casa Comiendo, invited me to one of his favourite restaurants. His family owns a vineyard in Mendoza so he's really into wine. But the evening was a good confidence boost for me and the opposite of the dating app disaster.'

She was babbling, but she couldn't admit to her daughter that she'd gone home with Felipe, and she didn't want Eva to get the wrong idea about them. It wasn't like she and Felipe were going to see each other again. They were just friends and colleagues.

Nothing to explain.

Colleagues who'd had passionate and steamy sex. *Twice.* Her stomach quivered at the memories.

Eva looked up from slicing tomatoes and capsicums with surprise. 'So you're *not* seeing him again?' Her mouth turned down in a frown of disappointment.

'No, apart from at work.' Emilia shook her head and stole half a cherry tomato from the chopping board, popping it into her mouth, a twinge of regret pinching her stomach. 'We're just friends. He's a committed bachelor who's been casually dating for fifteen years since his divorce, so I desperately needed his advice on how to spot a bad date after my first disaster.'

Funny that they hadn't talked much about dating tips though. They'd been too busy sharing stories of the places they'd travelled and the books they liked and the movies they wanted to see. And now that she'd taken that terrifying leap and overcome her fear of being intimate with another man, maybe the next time she wanted to be social she could embrace online dating once more.

She sighed. Meeting a random stranger still held little appeal.

'Oh…' Eva looked away. 'Well at least you're actually putting yourself out there, Mamá. I'm proud of you. I know it's not easy. But surely the first few dates are the hardest. You'll soon get into the swing of it.'

Emilia's heart sank. Eva obviously still expected her to persevere with the wretched dating app. Emilia hadn't expected that meeting new men would be *easy*. Except with Felipe, of course. It had been such a relief to go out with someone honest and mature and with no hidden agenda. Not to mention sexy as sin. And today had proved that their insanely passionate night wasn't going to affect their working relationship in the slightest. She should feel relieved, and she did, but there was also a wistful edge to her thoughts, most likely due to how comfortable she felt around him.

Now she needed to keep her hands off him at the hospital.

'So, what about you?' Emilia asked, trying to change the subject so Eva wouldn't worry about her sad, single mother. 'Any social plans in the pipeline?' Since starting UBA, Eva had only mentioned a couple of friends. Emilia knew it took time to settle in and find your tribe, but she couldn't help but worry after the upheaval of moving to a new country and leaving behind all her old friends.

'Actually, yes,' Eva said, tossing her long hair over one shoulder. 'I'm hanging out with Paloma at the weekend, a girl I met at volleyball.'

'Oh, that's great.' Emilia's heart swelled with pride. 'I'm so glad that you're making new friends.'

Eva shrugged. 'Paloma lives on campus, and

there's a party for first years at the student's association. We might swing by.'

'Great,' Emilia said, her stomach clenching painfully at the idea of Eva leaving home like her peers. She wanted the best for her daughter, of course. Eva needed to live her own life and not worry so much about her mother. But Emilia couldn't help the secret stab of loneliness that crept up on her. Her little girl was a woman. She'd soon be flying the nest, and Emilia would have to get used to living all alone.

Her breath caught on a wave of grief. Ricardo should be there. They were supposed to grow old together after their daughter was all grown up. Just because Emilia had had sex again didn't mean all of her problems were miraculously resolved.

'If I'm out this weekend, perhaps you should organise another *real* date,' Eva suggested, sliding the salad ingredients into a bowl from the chopping board. 'That way you won't be at home by yourself.'

Emilia smiled, forcing herself to practice her brave face for when the time came for Eva to leave home. 'I don't mind being alone, *mija*, but you're right,' she added, seeing the look of concern on Eva's face. 'Maybe I will.'

Maybe now that she'd dispensed with her nerves over the whole dating thing, now that Felipe had provided a frame of reference for comparison, she could move on to more dating successes. The trouble was that Felipe Castillo had certainly set the gold standard. Their non-date date would be a tough act to follow.

For the rest of the week following his date with Emilia, a busy routine developed. Felipe's team were on call, which meant sleepless nights, several emergency surgeries and plenty of new surgical admissions. He and Emilia had spent hours together, operating and reviewing patients, building on their growing friendship.

However, every time they had five minutes alone in the surgical staff room, there was a palpable tension between them—knowing looks and the accidental and electrifying brush of a hand. It was driving him insane. There'd been no time for any more heated kisses though, and he should be okay with that sad state of affairs. Except Felipe couldn't seem to scrub their night together from his mind, nor could he convince himself that it would be foolish to do it again.

It was torture.

That Friday, on their final surgery of the day, Felipe and Emilia worked on a patent ductus arteriosus—or PDA—case.

'Do you have a good view?' Felipe asked, retracting the thoracotomy incision in the left third intercostal space to expand the surgical field.

'Thank you,' she said.

He glanced at Emilia across the table. Only her eyes were visible between her mask and her theatre hat, but now that he knew her so much better he could read her emotions in her stare. Their mutual professional trust and respect were obvious.

Operating together they'd quickly learned each other's preferred style. While Emilia was now performing simple routine surgeries unsupervised, they were still doing the more complex cases together. This routine heart surgery to close a PDA, an abnormal connection between the aorta and the pulmonary artery, would be relatively straightforward, but Emilia seemed a little tense.

'Adjust the light, please,' she asked the theatre technician, who angled the overhead light, directing the beam into the wound.

'So we have the aorta and pulmonary artery trunk,' she said, pointing out the major blood vessels to and from the heart. 'The vagus nerve and recurrent laryngeal nerve.'

Taking a forceps and scissors, she carefully opened the pericardium, the sac around the heart, to expose the abnormal connection. The structure normally closed soon after birth, but in cases where it remained patent, the mixing of oxygenated blood form the aorta and deoxygenated blood from the pulmonary artery placed undue strain on the heart and lungs.

'Haemostatic clip, please,' Emilia asked, reaching for the forceps while Felipe watched, confident now in her abilities. She was a meticulous surgeon. Careful and thorough. He had no concerns about her competence.

She isolated the fistula and placed two metal clips across the ductus.

'Looking good,' Felipe said, letting her know that he used exactly the same technique.

She'd finished sewing the pericardium closed when the cardiac monitor sounded an alarm. All eyes swivelled to the heart monitor, which spewed out a paper rhythm strip.

'Looks like sinus tachycardia,' the anaesthetist said with a frown of concern.

'Blood pressure?' Emilia asked, checking the operative field for evidence of haemorrhage or other serious complications.

'BP looks good,' the anaesthetist confirmed, silencing the alarm.

'I can't see any bleeding or pneumothorax,' she said, her worried stare meeting Felipe's. 'Am I missing something?'

It was natural to doubt yourself when those alarms sounded. They were designed to prompt action in an emergency. Only that sometimes there was no obvious explanation for an elevated heart rate.

'I don't think so.' He shook his head, repeating the same checks that Emilia had made. Cardiac arrhythmias were relatively common in neonates, and this one didn't appear to be associated with hypovolaemic shock, which would indicate blood loss.

'Are you happy for us to close?' Felipe asked the anaesthetist, quickly shaking off the false alarm. He tried to communicate reassurance to Emilia through his eyes, but she seemed intent on checking again. For some reason, despite her assuring him she had no regrets, Felipe sensed an extra tension between them today.

At the all-clear, Emilia resumed the surgery, closing the chest and siting a drain in the pleural space to prevent the build-up of any air or fluid around the lung.

'Well done,' Felipe said as they left Theatre. 'I couldn't have done that better myself. One more week of supervision and you'll be all set to go it alone.'

He wanted to reassure her that he had no professional hesitations when it came to her surgical abilities, that the two of them succumbing to their mutual attraction would in no way affect his recommendation for her full registration with the

Argentine Medical Council. Only he'd kind of assumed that it went without saying.

'Thanks,' she said, tossing her gown and hat into the laundry bin and heading for the sink. 'Nothing like an alarm to keep you on your toes, keep your adrenal glands working.'

'The perfect end to a long and busy week.' He smiled as he flicked on the taps and began sluicing his hands and arms with water. 'So, any plans for the weekend?' he asked, keeping his tone light. He was fishing, yes, and he didn't want her to feel as if she had to tell him about her personal life. Only a big part of him wanted to ask her out again. They could take the dogs to the park, stop for an ice cream, perhaps catch that new movie they both wanted to see.

Except they were together all the time at work, and neither of them had suggested a repeat of that night. Maybe for Emilia one night had been enough.

'Um…well, Eva is going to a party on campus with a new uni friend,' she said, focusing on washing her hands and not looking at him. She yanked a couple of paper towels from the dispenser and dried her hands. 'And I'm…um… going on another date tomorrow, actually.' She looked up at last and sheepishly met his stare. 'I thought I'd give the app one more try.'

Felipe swallowed down his jealousy and disappointment, plastering a bland expression on his face. 'Sounds good. But is everything okay? You seem a little tense.'

She sighed and shrugged, turning to lean back against the sinks with her arms crossed over her chest. 'Well, I'm not really looking forward to meeting another stranger to be honest. And I guess I feel a little awkward discussing it with you, after…' She tilted her head. '…you know.' She glanced down the deserted corridor, ensuring they were alone.

Oh, *he* knew exactly what she meant. They'd agreed it was a one-off, but the part of him that still fancied her like crazy, that frequently relived every minute of their night together, couldn't forget how good they'd been. He didn't want to hear how she was dating another man.

But he also wanted her to be happy. She *deserved* to be happy after everything she'd been through. Who knew, perhaps her *Mr Right* was out there waiting for her.

'No need to feel awkward,' he said, tossing his balled-up paper towels in the bin with a little too much force. The idea of there being a *Mr Right* for Emilia shouldn't bother him. He'd happily abandoned the idea of being that for anyone many years ago. Perhaps it was just Thiago's looming wedding putting romance in the air.

'I too have a date tonight, as it happens,' he

said, leaning beside her, his shoulder a few inches from hers. 'I arranged it weeks ago.' He held her stare. He had no idea why that last detail was important, especially as they weren't seeing each other and she also had a date, but he wanted her to know that he'd organised his date *before* they'd slept together.

'Oh…' Her face coloured and she looked away. 'That's great. Are you going anywhere special?'

Did he imagine her flash of disappointment? Was she jealous, too? Maybe they should both admit that this wasn't over and date each other again. Only that seemed…complicated.

One, she didn't really want to date and was only doing it for Eva. Two, they were colleagues and needed to keep *them* a secret. And three, Felipe rarely dated the same person more than two or three times. Longer represented something serious, and he'd spent the past fifteen years shying away from that. It was just that he'd never met anyone he got along with as well as Emilia.

'Just drinks,' he said with a casual shrug. 'Maybe dancing if it goes well.' Although he'd much rather take Emilia dancing. But he owed it to tonight's date to make an effort.

'Well,' she said, as they headed for the theatre changing rooms, 'I took your advice about only meeting for drinks. Even so, I'm a little nervous about meeting another complete stranger. But that's normal, right?'

'Of course,' he said, his voice full of reassurance as they paused outside the staff changing rooms. She was going out with another man, but he still wanted her to have a good time and feel confident, and she still clearly needed his *dating coach* advice. Only witnessing her uncertainty, he also wanted to take her in his arms, hold her, whisper words of encouragement until she smiled that beautiful smile of hers. But she was a grown woman. She didn't need him to hold her hand no matter how badly he wanted to.

'Just be yourself and have a good time,' he said, forcing himself to inch towards the male changing room on the left. 'I'll see you Monday.'

'You too,' Emilia called, her smile looking a little forced as she ducked through the opposite door marked *female*.

Inside the changing room, Felipe yanked off his scrubs and slammed open his locker, frustration an itch under his skin. He had no right to feel jealous. He and Emilia weren't exclusive, or even dating. *He* definitely wasn't her *Mr Right*. He should be looking forward to his own date tonight. The woman was a successful accountant with a love of good wine and a divorcee, like him. They had heaps in common.

Except she wasn't Emilia.

CHAPTER TEN

THAT SATURDAY EVENING Felipe met with Thiago in Bar Armando, a popular casual bistro not far from the hospital. They had heaps of wedding plans to discuss, including Felipe's important role as best man. Only all Felipe could think about was Emilia. She'd even been on his mind last night, throughout his decidedly average date with the accountant.

Jealousy soured his mouth, so when the barman placed two tall, sweating glasses of golden beer on the table, he barely even noticed. Somewhere, right now, out there in the city, Emilia was meeting another man. Was she okay? Still nervous? Having a horrible time? He had the irrational idea to text and check in with her, before he pulled himself together and focused on his brother.

'So, I'm giving you the rings now,' Thiago said, handing over two velvet boxes. 'Obviously remembering to bring them to the ceremony next weekend is your most important job.'

Felipe pocketed the ring boxes and took a sip of

beer, trying and failing to forget about Emilia. 'I thought my most important job was to tell embarrassing stories about you in my best man speech.'

Thiago shook his head and ignored the jibe. Felipe grinned, looking up from his brother to see Emilia enter the bar. His smile slid from his face while his heart went crazy. She looked sensational in a sexy black dress with a low back.

Then, his stomach dropped. He watched as if in slow motion as she approached the busy bar. She was meeting her date there, at Bar Armando. He felt as if he'd been punched in the gut, but he couldn't look away as Emilia greeted a guy wearing a shiny grey suit who'd been sitting at the bar when Thiago and Felipe had arrived ten minutes ago.

The man appeared to be on his third or fourth shot already, and he didn't even stand up to greet Emilia properly. He simply waved his hand at a vacant barstool, motioning for Emilia to join him.

Felipe fumed on Emilia's behalf. What a jerk. She deserved so much better.

He'd completely zoned out of the wedding talk, barely hearing his brother's comments on the burgeoning guest list and the hire company they'd engaged for the extra tables and seating required.

His insides twisted with jealousy as he watched Emilia order a glass of wine and then turn her lovely smile on her date. Stupid, because he and

Emilia weren't a couple. They weren't exclusive. They weren't even dating. They were just friends, and like Felipe she was free to see whoever she chose. Except, his feelings didn't seem to give a damn about any of that. *He* wanted to be the one on a date with her tonight. *He* wanted to pull out her chair and offer her his arm and kiss her goodnight.

Disgusted with the possessive direction of his thoughts, Felipe knew he shouldn't watch her date unfold. But his stare was glued to Emilia. She'd only just sat down, but the creepy guy in the shiny suit kept touching her—her arm, her hand, even her bare shoulder—and she clearly wasn't into it. Felipe could see her flinch away from this distance.

'…and the band we wanted has become free so Violetta is excited, but—' Thiago finally broke off, the sudden silence drawing Felipe's attention away from the woman who'd occupied his thoughts since the moment they'd met.

'That's fantastic,' he said, faking it, one eye on his brother and the other on Emilia.

The man she was with slid his stool closer, leaning in to whisper something in her ear. Felipe looked down, feeling nauseous. He had no claim to her. He himself had gone on a date last night, as previously arranged. And while the woman he'd met had been perfectly nice and clearly only interested in dating casually, he hadn't even taken her up on her offer to go back to her place. It was as if now that he'd slept with Emilia his heart wasn't interested in dating anyone else.

'You haven't heard a word I've said for the past five minutes,' Thiago complained. 'Have you?'

Felipe winced and fought the urge to check on Emilia again. 'Of course I have. The band. Great news.'

Thiago scowled, unimpressed. 'Don't pretend that you've been listening.' He jerked his chin in the direction of the bar. 'Who is she anyway?'

'Who is who?' Felipe said, playing dumb as he stared down at his drink without taking a sip.

Thiago grinned, knowingly. 'The beautiful woman you can't keep your eyes off. I assume you know each other, perhaps intimately if the daggers you're shooting at the man she's with are any indication.'

Felipe waved his hand, evasively. 'We work together. She's a fellow consultant at the General, and my sex life is none of your business, baby brother.'

Thiago raised his hands in surrender and relaxed back in his seat, wearing *that* look on his face. A younger brother knew exactly how to needle on older one, and vice versa. 'If you're so hung up on her, old man, why is she over there fending off that idiot, while you're over here, mooning and lovesick?'

Felipe kept his face impassive, no mean feat considering he wanted to tie the touchy-feely hands of Emilia's date behind his back with his own shiny tie.

'I'm not lovesick,' he said. 'I'm just looking out for her, that's all. She's just moved here, and she's been single since she lost her husband five years ago. She's new to dating, and there are some real creeps out there.'

He glanced Emilia's way once more, appalled to see that the guy she was with was now knocking back red wine and talking about himself loudly, drawing attention.

'Maybe *you* should be the one dating her,' Thiago said, smugly. 'That way you can save her from the creeps and also focus on an important conversation with your one and only brother.'

'Sorry,' Felipe said, resolutely turning his back on Emilia. 'I *am* listening, I promise. The wedding—I can't wait.'

But Thiago had made an excellent point. Why couldn't he and Emilia continue to date, in secret, of course? After all, Felipe's last date had been as tedious as Emilia's current one seemed to be. Perhaps what they needed was to casually date each other until this thing between them fizzled out. It made perfect sense.

Thiago shook his head dismissively. 'Okay, cut the sarcasm. I hope you're going to put on a better show of enthusiasm than this on the day of the wedding, if only for the sake of my bride. Perhaps you should invite your friend over there to be your plus one,' he suggested. 'You might actually enjoy the event then…'

Felipe froze, a thrill snatching at his breath. Why hadn't he thought of that? It was the perfect solution. Not only would he love to have Emilia's easy and enjoyable company at the wedding, but he could also show her the family vineyard. Not to mention that her presence as his *date* would deflect the inevitable questions from well-meaning relatives about Felipe's long-time single status.

'That's not a bad idea actually…' he said slowly, thinking it through.

Emilia would have no expectations of their date. She'd made it clear that, like him, she wasn't interested in anything serious. They could just focus on their friendship and having a good time—dance a little, sample some world-class wines, enjoy the stunning setting of Mendoza's Uco Valley where he'd grown up. He'd wine her and dine her and put that smile back on her face. Everyone loved a good wedding.

'I do have them from time to time,' Thiago said dryly.

Felipe checked his watch, wondering how long

it might be until he could invite her to the wedding as his plus one, deciding he'd give it until her date with the creep was over, but not a second more.

Emilia abandoned her unfinished wine, fixed her tense smile in place and ducked her shoulder yet again from underneath her date's over-familiar and slimy touch. 'Well, thanks for meeting up. I think I'll be going now.'

She'd forced herself to try another date tonight, predominately for Eva. And she'd also wanted to prove to herself that she could have a good time without Felipe guiding her through the process. But no matter how hard she'd tried to make the effort, this guy, Marco, was definitely no Felipe Castillo.

'Don't go,' Marco whined, rudely clicking his fingers to attract the attention of the barman. 'Let's have another drink.'

'Not for me, thanks,' Emilia said, pushing back her barstool and clutching her bag like a shield. She should never have sat down. Marco had been drunk when she'd arrived, and during their brief conversation he'd also downed most of a bottle of red wine. She'd only stayed for the half a drink she'd managed out of some warped sense of politeness. But she couldn't tolerate a second longer of his loud and obnoxious company, not to mention the vile pawing.

She shuddered, sliding from her barstool—she was going straight home for another shower.

'Of course you will,' Marco said, rudely ignoring her as he summoned the barman over. 'Another bottle of red, please,' he said to the young guy. 'And a fresh glass for the lady.'

Emilia caught the barman's eye and shook her head, inching away between the cramped barstools so no part of her accidentally brushed against Marco.

'Is everything okay?' the barman asked Emilia, ignoring Marco's order.

'Yes, thanks,' she said, clenching her jaw with determination. 'I'm just leaving.' She hadn't signed up for *this*. She wanted a little fun, some light-hearted company, maybe a little flirtation, not to run the gauntlet of lecherous creeps who thought themselves entitled to sex simply because she'd shown up.

'No,' Marco cried, coming to his feet and swaying slightly. 'We haven't swapped numbers. I want to see you again, unless you want to get out of here now, together.' He raised his eyebrows hopefully.

'No,' Emilia said firmly. 'I'm leaving, *alone*.'

'She's not interested, mate,' the barman said

quietly to a belligerent Marco. 'Don't make a scene.'

Emilia was about to turn away and head for the exit when Marco turned on the young barman.

'Mind your own business and get my wine,' he spat, raising his voice so several people turned to stare.

Emilia hesitated, her face aflame. She wanted to escape this disastrous date, but she couldn't abandon the young barman who'd come to her rescue. He didn't look much older than Eva, and Marco had now turned the full force of his disgruntlement onto him.

Before she could intervene, someone touched her elbow. She was so jumpy, she yelped. But it was Felipe.

She almost sagged with relief to see a friendly face.

'Are you okay?' he asked, guiding her a short distance away while the bar staff dealt efficiently with the drunken Marco, escorting him outside to hopefully put him in a taxi.

Emilia nodded, touching Felipe's arm with gratitude. She was so pleased to see him. 'I'm fine,' she lied, feeling close to tears. 'He'd had too much to drink.' She sniffed, glancing down while she tried to manage her humiliation. 'It seems my third date was even worse than the first one. You promised me they would get better.' She forced herself to smile and met his compassionate stare, dragging her eyes away from the open neck of his shirt and the tantalising glimpse of dark chest hair and golden skin.

She shouldn't drool over one man while her date with another was barely over. But even if Marco had been sober and charming, she wouldn't have given him her number or agreed to a second date. They'd had zero sexual chemistry, unlike her and Felipe...

'For me, the bad dates seem to outnumber the one good one,' she said with a humourless laugh. 'You must tell me your secret.' No doubt his date last night had been a resounding success, especially if he'd looked even half as hot as he did tonight. But she couldn't think of that, or she'd want to ask if he'd slept with the woman, if he planned to see her again, none of which was her business.

Felipe pressed his lips together and glanced over his shoulder, looking torn. Emilia stepped back, mortified. Was he on another date? A second date, perhaps, with the woman from last night, because it had gone so well. Oh, no....

Not only had Felipe witnessed Emilia's *date from hell*, but she'd probably also dragged him away from some glamorous and entertaining beauty. It was Saturday night after all.

'I'll be fine,' she blurted, desperate now to run home. 'Don't let me interrupt your evening. I'm going to wait until he's definitely gone—' she glanced at the door '—and grab a taxi.'

'Look,' Felipe said with a frown, his hand lingering on her bare elbow, which was enough contact to send her entire body up in flames, despite her humiliation. 'I'm having a drink with my brother. Why don't you come and say hello.'

Emilia nodded, too confused by the relief coursing through her veins to speak. So he *wasn't* on a date. Should she be this relieved? Except Felipe hadn't simply set the standard against which her other dates could be measured, he'd also set Emilia's expectations sky high.

But why shouldn't she hold out for a kind, smart and thoughtful mature man who was also a great lover? At her age and stage in life, she absolutely refused to settle.

'Thiago,' Felipe said as the other man stood, 'this is Emilia Gonzales. We work together at the General. Emilia is from Uruguay.'

Emilia shook Thiago's hand. He looked just like his handsome older brother, the same deep brown eyes, only with longer hair.

'Nice to meet you,' she said, feeling less self-conscious than if Felipe had been with another woman, although his brother had likely witnessed her terrible date, too. 'I hear you're soon to be married. How are the preparations going?'

Thiago smiled a charming smile. 'I'm largely

keeping out of the way, as any sensible groom would. But I'm looking forward to it. Having hosted so many other people's weddings at Castillo Estates it will be great to enjoy my own wedding there.'

'Why don't you join us for a drink?' Felipe urged, smiling, his hand sliding to the small of her back—she shivered with delight rather than revulsion, as she had at that other man's touch. Thiago nodded in agreement.

'Oh, no, thanks.' Emilia blinked, her eyes stinging again, this time with emotion at their kindness. The Castillo family had raised two exceptional sons. 'That's very kind, but I'm heading home, now.'

Confused by her reaction to Felipe's touch, she wanted to hurl herself into his arms, to feel safe and respected. They were so good together. But she needed to remember that, A, they were just friends and colleagues and, B, Felipe was a committed bachelor, himself still dating other people. She couldn't rely on him for emotional support, no matter how tempting.

'Then let me see you home,' Felipe said, stepping closer and lowering his voice. 'You seem understandably shaken up.'

Emilia fought the urge to beg him to hold her, to feel his strength surround her, to hear his murmured reassurances as she had that night they'd slept together, when he'd been so considerate of her feelings and treated her like he truly cared. Instead, she vigorously shook her head and backed away from the dangerous temptation of him. 'No, please don't interrupt your evening on my account. I'll be fine. Eva will probably be back from her party and waiting for me at home, anyway.'

Felipe likely *did* care. He was a considerate person. But they weren't a couple, only friends who'd slept together. No doubt there was some new fandangle term for that, but the important thing was that she was fine alone.

She swallowed, a new resolve straightening her spine. 'It was a good thing that my date was a disaster, actually. It's helped me to decide that I'm absolutely done with dating apps.'

Felipe frowned in concern and Thiago winced.

'Enjoy the rest of your night,' she said, smiling as brightly as she could manage before heading for the door.

Outside the cool breeze caressed her heated face. What a horrible evening, the humiliation of her date made more obvious by the contrast of Felipe's soothing presence, not that she'd needed rescuing. It was only that for a second, when he'd first touched her arm, it had felt so good to have an ally, to know that she hadn't been as utterly alone as she'd often felt these past five years.

But one thing was certain—she wasn't putting

herself through any more mystery dates, not even for Eva. She'd meet someone the old-fashioned way or not at all.

CHAPTER ELEVEN

LATER THAT NIGHT, after saying goodbye to his brother, Felipe tapped on Emilia's front door. He took another glance at his phone and the text he'd received in response to his, which had enquired if she'd made it home safely and how she was feeling.

I'm okay. Eva is staying the night at her friend's place. Come over and keep me company if it's not too late.

After witnessing her demoralising date tonight, wild horses couldn't have kept him away. She didn't need him to look out for her, but he hated the idea that she might be feeling vulnerable and alone. Seeing her out with another guy tonight, all dressed up and hopeful only to be so badly let down, had sent his protective urges into overdrive.

They weren't an item, but he hadn't expected to feel so…jealous, so possessive and invested in her happiness. He'd even abandoned his beer and switched to soft drinks after Emilia had left the bar, just so he could drive to her place and check up on her.

The door swung open and she stood on the threshold. His heart thumped excitedly. She'd changed out of her dress into jeans and a sweater. She looked relaxed and welcoming and unbearably beautiful.

'Hey, how are you feeling?' he asked, leaning in to brush her cheek with a kiss.

'I'm good. Come in.' Her smile for him was just the ego boost he needed. It lit her eyes as if, right then, he was the only person she wanted to see.

But he was fantasising, and he couldn't afford to overthink his possessive feelings. They were understandable, as he'd said to Thiago, considering how well they got on and after everything Emilia had been through—losing her husband, raising their daughter alone and moving countries. And of course the amazing sex had complicated things, distorting his perspective.

Felipe followed her into a modern living room filled with comfy sofas, contemporary furniture, lamps and potted houseplants. A dog, he assumed Luna, greeted him with a thumping tail before sloping back off to her faux-fur dog bed.

'Coffee or wine?' Emilia asked, the wide neck of her sweater slipping to reveal one tanned and freckled shoulder and the lacy strap of her bra.

'Better make it coffee. I drove here.' Felipe released an internal groan of frustration. He was so drawn to her brand of effortless sophistication and unassuming sex appeal. Only he'd come to support her, not to seduce her. But resisting her now that they'd been intimate and knew each other so much better would not be an easy task, especially if she kept looking at him in *that* way.

'Thanks for coming over,' she said as she prepared his coffee. 'I think I was still a little in shock when you texted. When I got home to find Eva's message and an empty house, I almost burst into tears. Thank goodness for Luna.' She glanced gratefully at the dog, who thumped her tail in response.

'I'm sorry you had such a bad experience tonight,' he said, removing his jacket and taking the cup of coffee from her. 'Although you handled yourself impeccably. You were firm and classy. But forget about that guy. He wasn't worth your time,' he added as they sat side by side on the sofa.

Emilia had obviously been sitting there before he arrived. Her half-full glass of wine sat on the coffee table next to an open book. Felipe placed his mug on a coaster and turned his attention to Emilia, taking her hand in his. 'Are you truly okay?'

She nodded, vulnerability clouding her stare. 'But I just can't do it any more,' she said with a shudder. 'I was going through the motions of dating for Eva's sake. Ever since her father died, she worries so much about me being alone, and the last thing I want is to be any sort of burden to her. I want her to be young and carefree like her contemporaries.'

'Of course you do.' Felipe nodded in understanding even as he processed his disappointment that she was done with dating. 'You're a wonderful mother. A role model, not a burden. I'm sure your strength is inspiring to her.'

She blinked, gratitude shining in her eyes. Her fingers curled tighter around his. 'Thanks Felipe. What would I have done without you these past couple of weeks?'

Felipe's heart soared that she valued his friendship, except a huge part of him wanted to be more than her friend. Was that just his over-protectiveness at play? He still wasn't looking for a serious relationship, but that smile of hers was addictive. He wanted to be the man to put it on her face.

'I'm sorry that you've been unlucky with your dates,' he continued, sliding his thumb back and forth over the back of her hand—touching her was second nature. 'You deserve so much better. It's not supposed to be *that* hard.'

And if she was finished with dating, where did that leave them and his hopes that they could spend more time together?

'Right?' She nodded in agreement. 'I mean I'm not even looking for love. I've had that once.' Her eyes landed briefly on the framed photo on the table—her and Eva and a man that was obviously Ricardo. 'I was just hoping for a little fun,' she said, 'like the night *we* went out—nice food, great conversation, no games. That was easy. You made me feel uplifted. But I can't go through another date like tonight's. Not even for Eva. I know she'll be disappointed with me, but it's just not worth it.'

She looked down at their clasped hands and compassion swelled in his chest. He would be her friend if that was all she wanted.

'She'll understand,' he said, resting his index finger under her chin and tilting it up so their eyes met. 'You two are wonderfully close. But the downside is that you know each other so well emotionally. Talk to her and explain how you feel. Just because you're not ready to date now, doesn't mean you won't be one day.'

Although a huge part of him had hoped she might want to date *him* again…

She nodded and glanced at the photo once more. 'Eva and I *are* close. Losing her father hit her so hard. She was very withdrawn for a long time.' She sighed and Felipe squeezed her hand. 'Of course, I worry that I'm messing her up even more because I'm the only parent she has now…'

Felipe shook his head adamantly. 'I'm no expert when it comes to teenagers, but if it's any reassurance, she seems like a very intelligent and switched on young woman.'

A soft smile touched her lips. 'Thanks for listening, Felipe.' She snagged her bottom lip with her teeth, drawing his attention back to those soft, kissable lips. 'Sometimes I forget that Ricardo isn't here. I'll have a bad day at work or a parental worry and my first thought is to discuss it with him. Then, with sickening shock, I remember that he's gone and that, whatever the dilemma, I need to deal with it alone. It sounds silly, but it can be so tiring.'

'Not silly at all.' Felipe took her hand in both of his, his offer spoken before he could overthink the impulse. 'I know it's not the same, but you can call me any time and I'll listen, help out if I can. I'm alone too, so I get it, only I don't have the responsibility of a child of my own. But seriously, just call me.'

'That's very thoughtful of you.' She blinked and swallowed as if struggling to find the words. 'I hope I didn't ruin your evening, too. What must your brother think of me?'

Felipe made a dismissive sound, wishing he could hold her in his arms, kiss her and chase away all her fears and doubts. But she was strong. And fortunately she didn't need him to take care of her, because he was no good at that.

'I'm not particularly happy about him noticing,' he said about Thiago, 'and I let it slide because he's getting married, but he thought you were beautiful, which you are.' He grinned, partly joking about his brother and partly serious. It seemed where Emilia was concerned, the possessive feelings, the jealousy, no matter how unfounded, were here to stay.

She stared, her eyes flicking between his as the tension between them seemed to crackle. Oh, how badly he wanted to seduce her again, to show her just how beautiful and amazing she was, to worship her body with his until he'd replaced her humiliation from earlier with memories of passion. But he needed to tread carefully. Emilia was feeling understandably vulnerable and alone, and he'd really only come here to check on her. She didn't need a saviour and he couldn't be one. He was no longer serious commitment or husband material.

'Tell me more about Ricardo,' he said instead as he glanced at the picture of them together, steering the conversation out of danger and deliberately bringing up the man who *had* been everything to Emilia.

She eyed him curiously, some of the tension leaving her. 'You really want to know?'

'About the man you loved?' he asked. 'Sure.' Felipe didn't see Emilia's husband as competition. Strangely he wasn't jealous of Ricardo Gonzales. Their marriage and their history was theirs and theirs alone. He certainly wasn't looking to replace the man, even if he could have. It was just that Ricardo Gonzales had excellent taste in women.

'You might have liked him, actually,' Emilia said with a soft smile. 'He was a runner too. He completed the Montevideo marathon six times, before Eva came along.'

'Impressive.' Felipe nodded, urging her to continue. 'How did you meet?'

She relaxed back into the sofa and placed her other hand over his in her lap, so now his hand was sandwiched between both of hers. 'He was travelling after graduating from UBA. He was sleeping on the floor of a friend of mine before taking off to backpack around Brazil. I knew after our first date that he was *the one*, but we were also great friends.'

She smiled fondly. 'I'd been planning to go travelling too, so I changed my itinerary and we explored Brazil together. You really get to know a person when you share a two-person tent.'

Felipe smiled in agreement. 'I can imagine.'

Still clinging to his hand, her expression changed, as if she was no longer seeing the past, but was firmly in the present. 'Your brother looks a lot like you. Are you close?'

Felipe shrugged, relaxed in her company, as always. 'We are surprisingly close, although sometimes I overdo the protective big brother thing. He's a good man. I'm glad that he's met Violetta and that she makes him happy.'

Only Thiago's happiness and the wedding plans, combined with his jealousy over Emilia's date, had accentuated Felipe's restlessness, his loneliness. It was as if his career and his string of deliberately casual dates were no longer enough to keep him content. And the only thing in his life that had changed was him meeting Emilia.

'The family business sounds very successful,' she continued, dragging him away from the unsettling thought. 'How many weddings do you host a year?' She reached for her wine glass from the table and took a sip.

'I believe it was over thirty last year. Not that *I* can take any credit. The success is all down to Thiago.'

She eyed him over the rim of her glass, placing it back on the table. 'I've touched a nerve?'

While Emilia was a great listener, Felipe hesitated. 'Not really...' He didn't want to expose his worst flaws to this woman, but Emilia didn't play games. She wouldn't use his regrets against him, and she'd opened up to him about all sorts of things tonight.

'It's just that sometimes when I see Thiago,' he continued, 'I still feel a little guilty that I abandoned Castillo Estates to follow my surgical career. He's never thrown it back at me, but he had no choice in having to step up and take over the business from our parents after they retired.'

Emilia frowned, her dark stare full of empathy. 'We all have a choice, Felipe. Thiago doesn't strike me as a pushover. I'm sure that he'd have followed a different career if he'd really wanted one. Your parents could have employed a manager or sold the business.'

'That's true.' She was so understanding. 'I guess the guilt comes from in here.' He rested his balled-up fist over his sternum. 'So it's not particularly logical.'

She leaned closer, the passion building in her voice. 'Because you're a decent man who cares about people. But it's like my wise daughter says—*you* deserve to be happy too. It's okay to have your own ambition and dreams, and you've worked long and hard for your career.'

'Yes…'

She eyed him sadly. 'Yes, but…?' she pressed with a question in her voice.

Felipe dragged in a deep inhale. 'But I'm aware how my ambition, my career, has also cost me my marriage in addition to burdening my brother with the family business.' Why was he telling her this? It was as if she'd popped the lid on his deepest vulnerabilities and he couldn't seem to quell the outpouring.

Her stare softened with understanding. 'Nothing is ever that straightforward in a marriage,' she said, knowingly. 'It's the most complex and rewarding relationship we enter into. Two people, often from different walks of life, sharing everything—a home, a life, a family. Marriage takes work and commitment and compromise on both sides, and even then that's sometimes not enough to make it last.'

'Look at us,' he said with smile, hoping to lighten the mood—after all he'd come over to make her feel better. 'If only we'd had all this wisdom in our twenties.'

She chuckled. 'Indeed.'

Because he desperately wanted to kiss her, he raised her hand to his mouth and pressed a kiss there. 'Thanks for listening. I was supposed to be the one doing the comforting. That's why I came over.'

Emilia shrugged, her eyes bright. 'I like that it's mutual. And I can't take all the credit. You're easy to talk to, too. You make me feel safe and understood, so thank you.'

Felipe looked up from her mouth, his stare latched to hers. He didn't want to look away. He didn't want to miss one second of the way she was looking at him, because he recognised the desire in her expression and it matched the urgency pounding through him in time with his rapid heartbeat.

But he didn't want to cross the line.

'Your coffee's probably cold,' she whispered, her tongue touching her lush bottom lip.

'Who needs coffee?' He shrugged, willing her to make the first move, willing her to want him as much as he wanted her in that moment.

He couldn't promise her for ever, but he definitely wanted more than one night. They could have a good time while they continued to explore this intense chemistry.

It made so much sense. He just hoped she wouldn't take too much convincing.

CHAPTER TWELVE

EMILIA DRAGGED IN a shuddering breath as they stared at each other. She couldn't look away. That he'd driven over after his night out with his brother, that he'd not only listened to her express her concerns for Eva and talk about Ricardo, but also shared *his* feelings with her—it was humbling. At work, he was so controlled and driven and confident, she hadn't expected him to voice such deep-rooted doubts over his failed marriage and his relationship with his family.

He had so many positive attributes, but he was also a complex man with fears and regrets, just like her. The more time they spent together, the closer they became. And right then, the only thing she was certain of was how stupid it would be to ignore their continuing connection.

'You think I'm beautiful,' she whispered, her pulse tripping.

'I do,' he said, his grip tightening on her hand.

Silently, she leaned forward. He moved too and their lips met in a rush. Desperate, she whimpered. Felipe gripped her neck and her waist and commanded the kiss, which went from zero to ten in a second, as if they'd both been holding back for too long.

'I can't stop thinking about you,' he said, kissing a path down her neck as his hands slid inside her sweater to caress her skin. 'I can't stop wanting you.'

'Me neither,' she moaned, tilting her head to expose the sensitive places on her neck to his lips.

Why had she bothered with the dating app when she didn't even need to think about her relationship with Felipe? They just understood each other. Clicked. It was always easy, always uplifting and, if she was honest, she'd never stopped wanting him since the first time they were intimate.

'Come with me.' She stood, tugging him to his feet and leading him to her bedroom, closing the door to keep the dog out. They pulled at each other's clothes, their lips moving frantically together as they inched towards the bed, their tongues surging wildly to assuage the burning desperation of every touch.

This felt so right, it was almost terrifying. Only it wasn't about feelings or for ever. Felipe made her feel safe and accepted, so she could almost glimpse the old, resilient, grief-free Emilia, a woman who'd had it all: a husband she loved, a daughter, a career. Was that woman gone for ever, or was she there somewhere, licking her wounds, ready to one day make a comeback?

Because she was tired of thinking and wanted only to feel, she fumbled with Felipe's shirt buttons, exposing his bronzed chest, pressing her lips over his pecs and the valley between as her hands reached for his belt. She looked up as she stripped him. His stare was almost black with desire, as he removed her sweater and cupped her breasts, thumbing the nipples.

'I hated seeing you with him tonight,' he said, his voice breaking with the depth of his passion.

His jealously inflamed her, matching her own for the woman he'd taken out the night before. She crashed her lips back to his and slid her tongue into his mouth, as he unclasped and then removed her bra.

She didn't want to think about him being intimate with anyone else, even though she knew if he'd been single for fifteen years that he'd had his fair share of lovers.

Felipe gripped her upper arms and tore his mouth away. 'Ask me. I know you want to.'

She froze, her heart raging. She could pretend she had no clue what he was talking about. But what was the point? They were clearly frantic for each other.

'Did you sleep with her last night?' she asked,

her jealousy a shocking sting in her veins. She'd never been the possessive type and Felipe wasn't *hers*, but she wanted to know that he was as consumed with her as she was with him.

'No,' he said, hauling her lips back to his. 'I only want you.'

His dark head swooped and he captured her nipple between his lips, his tongue flicking over the bud. A deep ache settled in her belly. His hands unbuttoned her jeans as he sucked, pushing them over her hips until she'd wriggled free. Then he cupped her backside in both hands, grinding his erection between their bodies.

'Why haven't we been doing this all week?' she asked, slipping her hand inside his jeans.

She stroked him, smiling when he crushed her to his naked chest and groaned. 'I have no idea. Because we're stupid?'

Emilia laughed, pressed her lips over his neck, his jaw, his chest. Felipe fumbled with his wallet, removing a condom, and Emilia shoved at his jeans and boxers, sliding them over his hips so he could kick them off.

When he stood before her, gloriously naked and erect, and before he could put on the condom, she dropped to her knees and took him into her mouth. She wanted him as wild as she felt. She wanted to imprint the memory of tonight, of their undeniable passion, in both their minds. She wanted to banish any trace of her disastrous date and Felipe's previous lovers.

'Emilia,' he growled, watching her take him, his hands cupping her face, fingers tunnelling into her hair. 'You are so sexy.'

Power surged through her as his hips jerked and his skin flushed and his breathing turned harsh and ragged. He was so male—honourable and honest and trustworthy. He'd come to her rescue tonight in his own respectful way, not that she'd needed him. But it was good to know she wasn't totally alone, that she had a champion, someone on the same wavelength, someone who cared.

Before she could get carried away, he jolted his hips back and dragged her to her feet, kissing her soundly while he rolled on the condom and removed her underwear. His hands caressed her breasts as he walked her back towards the bed. She sat and he leaned over her, tonguing first one nipple and then the other. Emilia sighed, leaning back on her elbows as Felipe trailed the tip of his tongue down her body, until his mouth covered her sex.

She gasped, her head light with delirium, the waves of pleasure scalding her, hotter and hotter. 'Yes,' she cried, tunnelling her fingers through his hair as he worked her higher and higher, his hands splayed across her backside, holding her to his mouth.

Just when she thought she might come, he surged to his feet and covered her body with his, grasping one thigh over his hip as he pushed inside her.

'Look at me,' he said, entwining their fingers together as his hips moved in slow, deep thrusts.

Emilia held his stare, her body alive from his touch, her heart thudding against his as heat consumed her.

'I want to take you dancing, I want to pull out your seat and see you home safely,' he said, the sincerity in his stare a confirmation of Felipe's passionate nature.

'Yes…' Emilia nodded, chasing his lips with hers to satisfy the need burning her up.

He pulled back, his hips thrusting in a steady rhythm that took her higher and higher. 'I want to hold your hand and listen to your concerns and laugh with you.'

She nodded, too choked and turned on for speech. He was everything she needed in that moment, his words soothing her soul, his body driving her closer and closer to blissful release.

'I want you, Emilia,' he ground out, picking up the pace, shunting her higher and higher.

'Felipe,' she cried as her orgasm struck.

He kissed her, thrusting through every spasm until she was spent, and then he too let go, groaning against the side of her neck as his body stiffened in her arms.

Emilia held him as they each caught their breath, her heart a wild flutter behind her ribs and her throat tight with emotion. Their intense passion was difficult to deny, but after the emotional rollercoaster of the evening, now that they'd satisfied their physical need for each other, she wasn't sure how to feel apart from unsettled, as if she were being chased in the dark.

She lay still, her heart banging against his. This time had been different, more intimate, especially after their heartfelt talk.

But *nothing* had changed. They weren't making a commitment to each other. Felipe had managed to avoid serious relationships for fifteen years—Emilia was still very much focused on making sure Eva's life was stable, and was clinging to the precious memories of Ricardo. Not to mention that they worked together. If they didn't handle this physical side of their relationship like mature adults, it could damage their professional relationship when it ended. And given Felipe's commitment avoidance and her fear of opening up her emotions, it *would* end, probably sooner rather than later.

'Are you okay?' he asked, raising his head to peer down at her.

She nodded, still overcome by what tonight meant. 'I wasn't expecting that to happen.'

He offered her a small smile. 'Me neither, but we don't need to overthink it. You wanted me, I wanted you. We're both single.'

Emilia nodded, the simplicity of his explanation not quite dispelling her unease.

'I should go,' he said, pressing a soft kiss to her lips. His smile touched his eyes and she knew that he too was feeling a little caught off guard by what they'd just done. 'But first, I wanted to ask you something.' He rolled to the side and drew the covers over her body. 'Would you like to be my date at Thiago and Violetta's wedding next weekend?'

Emilia stilled, her heart racing with panic. A wedding date felt more serious than a regular date.

'We can make a weekend of it,' he added, perhaps sensing her hesitation. 'I'll even give you a personal tour of the estate, show you the vines and the cellar, and the very vat where I crushed my first vintage by foot when I was six years old.'

His excited smile was hard to resist. And where was the harm? He wasn't suggesting they become an item or even asking her to date him exclusively. As long as no one at the hospital got wind of it, it might be fun. A chance to dress up and dance and relax in a stunning part of Argentina, with a man who understood and respected her and had done so much for her confidence these past two weeks.

'I'd love to…' she said, chewing at her lip. 'But I don't know… I'd have to tell Eva if I'm away for the whole weekend, and I don't want to confuse her about us. Especially when I keep telling her that we're just friends.'

'Of course.' He nodded, the sparkle in his eyes dimming. 'We *are* friends, but I understand if it's too hard to explain. It's your call.'

Emilia touched his face, stroking her fingers through his luxuriant hair. 'Won't your family get the wrong idea, too? You said they're keen to see you settle down again. Won't me turning up as your date make them mistake us for a couple?'

That would only put pressure on the situation and *she* wasn't even sure herself what it was they were doing. *Friends with benefits? Casual sex? Secret fake dating?* It was all a messy blur.

Felipe took her hand and kissed the centre of her palm so her toes tingled. 'They know me well enough to understand that just because I bring along a date it doesn't mean I'm in a serious relationship. They know I'm done with those.'

Of course, his family knew him best. If he'd managed to stay single for fifteen years since his divorce, there was little risk of anyone, including Emilia, changing his mind.

'And anyway,' he added, 'it was Thiago's idea that I invite you. We can make it clear to anyone who asks that we're just friends.' He drew her lips back to him and pressed a whisper-soft kiss there, coaxing. 'Say yes. I want to show you where I grew up.'

Emilia dragged in a shuddering breath, berating herself. Felipe was a committed bachelor. It was much more likely that his family would see her as the *woman of the moment* rather than a serious contender for his heart.

'Okay. In that case, I'd love to go,' she said, ignoring the prickles of possessiveness that once more reared their head. So there would be lovers after her—that suited her just fine. If she wasn't ready to date strangers, she certainly wasn't ready to open her heart up to feelings. She might never be ready for that...

'But please don't mention that I'm going with you to anyone at work,' she urged. 'I don't want the hospital rumour mill to start up, and you *are* still my supervisor.'

After this fling or whatever it was ended, they still had to work together. Neonatal surgery was a small specialist field. They couldn't afford to allow their personal lives to damage the professional relationships they'd built up. And she highly valued his friendship. She wouldn't want to lose that either.

'Of course not,' he said with a small frown, stealing one last kiss before leaving her bed to deal with the condom.

They dressed and returned to the living room, collecting up the wine glass and coffee cup and stacking them in the dishwasher.

'I'll see you at work Monday,' Felipe said. 'We have that Hirschsprung's disease pull-through surgery first thing.' He drew her into his arms for another searing kiss that stole her breath. She'd barely released him when there was the sound of a key in the lock and Luna hurried into the hall, her tail wagging.

'Eva…' Emilia froze, staring in horror at Felipe, who was fully clothed but had that arousing post-sex look going on—tousled hair, rumpled shirt, slumberous eyes.

Panic snatched at her breath. What had she been thinking inviting him here? She could have met him at *his* apartment. She didn't want Eva to feel threatened or confused by her and Felipe's relationship. And aside from great sex, which was the one thing she *couldn't* discuss with her daughter, there really was nothing to tell.

Felipe nodded, stepped aside and ran his fingers through his hair while Emilia guiltily adjusted the neck of her sweater.

'Hello?' Eva called, appearing in the doorway with Luna a second later, her surprise at Felipe's presence evident.

'Mija, I thought you were spending the night at your friend's place,' Emilia said, praying that it wasn't obvious that her and Felipe had just got out of bed. 'You remember Felipe Castillo from the hospital, don't you?'

Her voice was too high pitched. She sounded guilty, as if she'd done something naughty. She took some calming breaths, reminded herself she was a grown woman who deserved a sex life, and forced herself to appear nonchalant.

'Hi,' Eva said to Felipe, barely looking his way as she tossed her bag on the sofa and stooped to give Luna an ear rub. 'Paloma's boyfriend came over,' Eva said, her voice flat with disappointment. 'I didn't want to play gooseberry, so I thought I'd leave them to it. Besides, I have heaps of studying to do tomorrow. I'm going to get up early and tackle my essay.'

'Oh…okay,' Emilia said, feeling flustered. 'Well, Felipe was just leaving. He rescued me tonight from a horrible date, but I'll tell you all about that tomorrow.'

'See you,' Eva said before heading towards her own bedroom with the dog in tow.

Emilia sighed, relieved that Eva hadn't suspected a thing, but also guilt-ridden that she'd been so careless. She crept outside onto the doorstep with Felipe, gently pulling the door behind her.

'That was close,' she said, wincing. 'Imagine if she'd come home five minutes earlier. How would I have explained that!' She'd have to be more careful. Her daughter was her priority, and she'd almost put herself and Eva in an embarrassing situation simply because she found Felipe Castillo irresistible.

Felipe frowned, a flicker of hurt in his stare, although she might have imagined it. 'It's okay for her mother to have a healthy sex life,' he said, gently raising her chin and kissing her softly. 'I'm sure she'd understand that you have your own life, your own needs.'

Emilia said nothing. The trouble was she wasn't a hundred percent convinced that it *was* okay for Eva to know those things, not when so much of her young life had been upturned by grief and confusion. Felipe wasn't Eva's father. Emilia certainly didn't want to discuss with her whatever it was that she and Felipe were doing, especially when they were just fooling around.

And what if Felipe was wrong? What if the idea of her mother with another man *did* upset Eva? What if she saw Felipe as some sort of threat for her mother's attention? What if she thought Emilia was trying to replace Ricardo? The poor kid had already been through so much. Emilia didn't want to put any kind of strain on their close relationship.

'Hmm,' she said, 'I'm not sure *I'm* ready for that particular parent–child conversation.' She knew he meant well, but they weren't a couple.

He accepted her excuse with a casual shrug, stepping back. 'Goodnight, Emilia, sleep well.'

'See you at work,' she said, holding onto his fingers until the last possible moment as he reluctantly stepped away and headed for his car.

She stayed on the doorstep to watch him leave, her head all over the place. Felipe's words rang through her mind. A big part of Emilia was scared to admit her own needs even to herself. Because admitting them meant acknowledging the hole in her life. She couldn't smother Eva, or live vicariously through her daughter, simply because she was too scared to open herself up to a fulfilling relationship. No one could replace Ricardo—she'd have to reiterate that to Eva. But did Emilia truly want to be alone for the rest of her life?

As she headed to bed, the scent of Felipe's cologne lingered on her sheets. Being brave enough to put her needs first and meet new people was one thing, but finding someone who she could connect with, trust and maybe open up her heart to was a whole other ballgame.

Even Felipe, who was head and shoulders above

those dating app guys she'd met recently, wasn't without risk. After all, he'd successfully and resolutely avoided a serious relationship and love for fifteen years.

Even if she wanted to, how could she put her bruised and terrified heart in the hands of a man like that?

CHAPTER THIRTEEN

EARLY MONDAY MORNING, at the request of his registrar, Felipe strode into the emergency department to review a new admission and saw Emilia already with the patient.

His blood heated at the sight of her, the memories of Saturday night as fresh as if she were still in his arms. They'd really opened up to each other that night. Her about her concerns for Eva's happiness, and him about his guilt over letting his family down. For a moment, as he lay in her bed, his heart pounding against hers, he'd felt so close to her.

Joining her now, excitement fizzed in his veins. He couldn't wait to show her off to his friends and family at the wedding that weekend. Of course, he'd need to downplay their relationship, as promised. He didn't want to upset her or spook her away with any awkward questions or misguided assumptions from his overzealous family.

Emilia looked up, spying him. Excitement flared in her dark eyes, gone in a blink. 'Good morning, Dr Castillo,' she said, with a tight, professional smile.

'Dr Gonzales,' he said, wishing he could kiss her breathless until she moaned his name. 'Who do we have here?' He glanced at the grizzling baby and the anxious parents expectantly.

'This is Bruno,' Emilia said. 'Two days old, born at thirty-nine weeks gestation by uncomplicated vaginal delivery. Bruno's parents became worried by a red swelling in the groin. He's pyrexial and not feeding, and on examination has an incarcerated left inguinal hernia.'

'Mind if I take a look?' Felipe asked the parents, quickly washing his hands at the sink.

Bruno's mother laid her fractious boy down on the bed, and Emilia and Felipe examined the newborn together as the parents worriedly looked on. As well as a painful, irreducible swelling in the left groin, Bruno also had a slightly distended abdomen and absent bowel sounds, all signs that a loop of intestine had become trapped inside the hernia, which required urgent surgical repair.

'As Dr Gonzales explained,' Felipe said, addressing the couple, 'it seems that Bruno has developed a small hernia.' He refastened the baby's nappy and handed him back to Mamá. 'The concern is that a piece of bowel is trapped inside the hernia. The longer it stays there the greater the risk that its blood supply is restricted. That can lead to necrosis of the bowel, so I'm afraid we need to surgically repair the hernia and, while we're there, have a look at the bowel to make sure it's all healthy. If we do find a necrosed segment of bowel, we'll also need to remove that, but this won't affect Bruno's ability to feed and grow as normal.'

'When did Bruno last feed?' Emilia asked as she and Felipe rewashed their hands.

'About eleven last night,' his mother said, 'but he also vomited some bile around five am.'

'We're about to head into Theatre,' Felipe explained, 'so we can add Bruno to our list and operate this morning. Dr Ruiz, my registrar who you've already met, will be along soon to consent Bruno for the surgery and run some blood tests.'

'The procedure shouldn't take more than an hour,' Emilia added, 'but we'll need to keep Bruno in hospital for a couple of days until he's feeding and his bowel starts working properly. You're welcome to stay with him, of course.'

'Any questions for us?' Felipe asked the couple, who glanced at each other and then shook their heads. 'Dr Ruiz can also answer any questions you think of after we've gone.' Felipe opened the curtains around the bed.

Emilia left the emergency department at his side, her demeanour somewhat distracted.

'Is everything okay?' he asked quietly as they headed for the surgery department.

'Fine,' she said, not quite meeting his eye. 'I came in early and saw Dr Ruiz. Thought I'd review the patient before Theatre in case he needed to be added to the urgent list for today, which as it turns out he does.'

Felipe nodded, frustrated that she was talking about work when he'd really been enquiring about *her*. 'I meant is everything okay with you?' He paused outside his office, inclining his head and inviting her in.

She hesitated for a split second and then followed him into the room. Felipe closed the door and immediately reached for her, scooping her into his arms as their lips met in a frantic breathy kiss of desperation. To his relief, she curled her arms around his neck and pressed her body against his. Felipe gripped her neck and deepened the kiss, his fingers curling into her hair as arousal flooded his veins.

'I missed you,' he breathed, pulling away from the kiss that had turned way more heated than he'd planned. He just couldn't seem to keep his hands off her, even at work.

Emilia shuddered, her eyes glazed with desire as she looked up at him. 'I missed you too... but we need to be careful. I don't want anyone to think that I didn't earn my job here, fair and square.'

Felipe winced—she was right. He didn't want to make her uncomfortable or let her down simply because he was crazy about her, and couldn't seem to keep his hands to himself.

'I'll try to control myself,' he said, stepping away. 'But there's nothing wrong with two colleagues talking before they head into a full day of surgeries. What happened after I left on Saturday? Was Eva suspicious because I was there so late?' he asked, wondering if concern for her daughter was the reason Emilia seemed a little out of sorts.

Emilia sighed. 'I don't think she suspected anything, which I'm relieved about. I know I'm entitled to a personal life,' she glanced down, 'but I don't want to do or say anything that might affect my relationship with her at the moment. She's still settling in at uni and trying to make new friends, she still misses her father terribly...'

It was the same message as Saturday night. Emilia obviously still had reservations about relationships. She clearly wasn't ready to put her own needs first, and Felipe could totally understand how she might be scared to upset her traumatised and vulnerable daughter.

That didn't stop the stab of doubt and disappointment though. He was so excited about her being his date for the wedding. He wanted to dance with her, show her the place he'd grown up, hold her all night long and sleep at her side. They would have the other person all to themselves for two whole days, a chance to really cement their growing connection.

'Did you tell Eva about the wedding invitation?' he asked cautiously, desperate for Emilia to commit to visiting Mendoza.

He wasn't a parent. He had no right to tell Emilia how to manage her relationship with Eva. And now clearly wasn't the right time to discuss them dating each other. Emilia was obviously holding back to focus on Eva, and he didn't want to push her further away. And part of him was terrified to over-commit, to give Emilia the wrong idea about them and hurt her. He wasn't sure where that left them—he just knew he wanted her.

'Yes, I did.' She looked down to where her hands were clasped together and his trepidation grew.

'How did she take it?' He didn't want to stop and analyse just how upset he'd feel if she changed her mind about being his date, especially when he wasn't offering her anything serious.

'She seemed okay about it.' Emilia frowned, obviously concerned and suspicious about Eva's reaction. 'She said that it sounded fun, and she hoped I'd have a great time,' she added, nibbling at her lip. 'I thought she'd be more pleased that I'm being social, but she was a little subdued. Perhaps she's stressed by her course workload.'

Hoping to appease her concerns, Felipe gripped her upper arms, pulling her close so she rested her head against his chest. 'You could always see how she seems as the week progresses. If you decide you need to stay at home with her, Thiago will understand. And I do too. Eva comes first.'

But the swoop of his stomach told him exactly how much he would miss her company now that the idea of her being his date had solidified.

'Thank you.' She looked up at him and blinked, the gratitude in her stare all the confirmation he needed about where Emilia's head was at, not that he could blame her.

He brushed her lips with his. 'That being said, I'd love you to be there as my date, but I also want you to have a good time and feel comfortable. You won't be able to do that if you're worried about Eva. Just let me know so I can book our flights to Mendoza.'

'I'm sure she'll be fine. She hates me fussing anyway.' Emilia smiled up at him, putting on a brave face. 'I'm really looking forward to the wedding. It will be nice to dress up and relax with you, and not have to rush home like I've missed my curfew.'

She kissed him again, her lips parting on a sigh and her tongue gently sliding against his.

His doubts disappeared. Just because there were complications, their relationship—their friendship and their physical connection—was important to him and, therefore, still worth pursuing.

Felipe lingered over their kiss, his mind snagged on how him and Emilia being together like this was bigger than just the two of them. It also involved the memory of Ricardo and the welfare of Eva. The ghost of his failed marriage and his fears of letting Emilia and Eva down. Their working relationship and their professional reputations. So much more at stake than simply two people having a good time.

And in many ways, he was wholly unprepared for such a complex relationship. He'd spent the past fifteen years avoiding serious entanglements, predominantly thinking only about himself. He needed to be so careful not to make Emilia any promises he couldn't keep. The last thing he wanted was to hurt her and, by extension, her daughter.

'That Hirschsprung's case is calling,' he said finally. 'We'd better head to Theatre. We have a busy day ahead.' Maybe they just needed to take their fling one day at a time. He would continue to support Emilia emotionally as her friend, without placing any pressure or expectations on her. It wasn't his place to interfere when it came to Eva anyway.

She nodded and stepped back, out of his arms. 'And I'm on call tonight, and you're on call tomorrow night.'

'Is there any chance we could get together mid-week after work?' Felipe asked, missing her already. 'I'm not sure I can wait until the weekend to be alone with you.'

Her sexy stare shone with mischief and promise. 'I'll see what I can do. Maybe I could sneak around to your place after work Wednesday night. Eva has a Modern Feminist's Society meeting, so I guess I could be a little late home without her noticing.'

'It's a date then,' he said, willing away every second of the next two days so he could kiss her freely. 'A *secret* date.'

Two days later, just as she was about to leave the General for the night and swing by Felipe's place as promised, Emilia was urgently called to the NICU to review Luis Lopez. The baby had been recovering well from his surgery, and had been weaned off his ventilator, but earlier today he'd taken a turn for the worse.

'He's been vomiting and passed some bloody stools,' Felipe's registrar Dr Ruiz said. 'His bloods are deranged and he's had a few apnoeic spells.'

Emilia examined the baby's abdomen, which was soft but slightly distended, her apprehension building. Her first instinct was to call Felipe, but he'd been on call last night and she could handle this without him, even if Luis was under their joint care. They weren't attached at the hip.

'Obviously the greatest concern is necrotising enterocolitis,' she told Dr Ruiz, fearful of the potentially life-threatening diagnosis, which comprised inflammation and bacterial overgrowth of the intestine. 'Let's stop the nasogastric feeds, start broad spectrum antibiotics and get an urgent abdominal X-ray,' she instructed the younger doctor.

The registrar made a note in the file. 'Dr Castillo has already left for the day,' he said, fatigue and concern in his eyes.

Emilia nodded, her poker face in place. She knew exactly where Felipe was. She was supposed to be at his apartment as they spoke. But kissing him, holding him, sharing her rough day with him would have to wait.

'I'll talk to the team on call tonight,' she said, 'and ask them to review Luis later this evening. Dr Castillo and I will review him first thing in the morning. Hopefully we can avoid surgery.' Although if the necrotising enterocolitis or NEC worsened, they might have to resect the involved segment of intestine.

Emilia asked Luis's neonatal nurse to contact Isabella and Sebastian. Then she turned back to

Felipe's registrar. 'Once you've ordered those tests, you should go home and get some rest. You were on call last night. I'll speak to his parents, let them know what's going on.'

By the time she'd checked the results of the abdominal film, which indeed confirmed distension and thickening of the bowel wall—the early stages of NEC—and had spoken to Isabella, Sebastian and the neonatal surgical team on call, it was close to eight p.m.

Herself tired after a long day, Emilia considered texting Felipe that she couldn't make it to his place and going straight home, but she wanted to see him. Eva had dropped a bombshell that morning about moving out, and Emilia was still reeling over the timing. She couldn't seem to shake the helpless feeling that her daughter was hiding something.

'I thought you'd changed your mind,' Felipe said with relief after swinging open the door to his apartment and reaching for her.

Emilia walked into his embrace and buried her face against the side of his neck, breathing his comforting masculine scent. 'I had to review Luis Lopez,' she said, looking up. 'He's developed stage one NEC.'

'Oh, no.' Felipe frowned and closed the door. 'Why didn't you call me? I'd have come back in.'

He guided Emilia inside his apartment and they sat on the sofa.

'Dr Ruiz and I dealt with it, and I've spoken to Jose,' she said about their neonatal surgical colleague, who was on call that night. 'He'll review him overnight and we can see him again first thing tomorrow. Hopefully he won't need a second surgery.'

Felipe nodded, his concerned frown lingering as his stare moved over her features. 'Are *you* okay? You seem…distracted.'

'I'm fine.' Emilia swallowed the sudden lump in her throat. He was so intuitive and thoughtful. 'Maybe I shouldn't have come. You must be tired after your on-call, but I wanted to see you.'

His smile softened. 'I'm glad that you came by. I'm not too tired for you.' He pressed his lips to hers and all of her troubles—work, Eva, the secrets she was keeping—seemed to dissolve. Only the taste of fear lingered. Was she too reliant on Felipe emotionally? It made sense after having to rely on him professionally while she was still under his supervision. But she couldn't lean on him the way she'd leaned on Ricardo. They weren't a couple, and a part of Emilia felt as if she had to shoulder her fears for Eva alone.

'Something else is wrong,' he said. 'Tell me what it is?' His stare offered the support she was scared to depend upon. Felipe was a wonderful doctor and a caring person, but he obviously enjoyed his carefree, single life. He didn't have his own children, and he had no need for the kind of committed, emotionally supportive relationship she'd had with Ricardo.

Except maybe she was overthinking it. He had said she could talk to him about anything…

'It's silly,' she said, resting her head over the thump of his heart.

'Tell me anyway,' he gently urged, his hands stroking her back.

Emilia surrendered with a small sigh. 'I'm just a bit thrown. This morning, Eva said she's thinking about moving out next semester. She wants to share a flat with some friends.'

She looked up and then away from the compassion in his eyes. 'She's finally had enough of living with her over-protective old Mamá.'

It was perfectly normal to outgrow your parents and want to be independent. Many of Eva's peers had already left home, but the house would be so quiet without her daughter. And Emilia would be truly alone, with only her memories for company.

Felipe tilted his head in sympathy, his palm cupping her cheek so she felt cherished and understood. 'Just because you care doesn't make you over-protective. I can understand how you must feel,' he said, brushing his thumb over her cheek, 'but leaving home is only natural. We've all been there.'

That he understood the complexities of having a grown-up child to consider and put first warmed Emilia's heart. Felipe would have made a wonderful father.

'I know.' She swallowed, her mind going to Ricardo. He'd always had a way of saying the right thing, too. What would he have thought of Felipe? And when had she started thinking of the two men in the same sentence?

But just because she needed a bit of support didn't mean anything. It was just a sign of how close she and Felipe had grown. No wonder, given they were working together and sleeping together and had become friends.

'No matter how much you prepare for your child leaving home,' she said, emotion straining her voice, 'when the time finally arrives it still feels as if it's crept up on you from nowhere, especially when it's your *only* child.'

Felipe drew her close and pressed his lips to the top of her head. 'You'll support Eva's decisions just as you've always done, but be gentle with yourself, okay?'

She nodded, snuggling back into his arms. It felt so good to lean on someone again, to share her troubles and not have to shoulder things utterly alone. Except what would she do when this came to an end? Would their friendship end too? Would she have to go back to hearing about his current date, or would they slowly stop confiding in each other and simply drift apart?

'Can you stay a while?' he asked, pulling back to press his lips to hers.

Oh, how she wished she could say yes and spend the evening with Felipe, cooking, eating, talking. But domestic bliss was something she'd only shared with her husband. Could she risk replacing those memories with new ones of her and Felipe, especially when their fling, their closeness, was obviously temporary?

Emilia shook her head. 'I'm sorry. Because I was delayed getting here, I really should get home now. I told Eva that I've given up on the dating app, so I've no excuse to be out late.'

She didn't want to tell Eva she was having a casual sex relationship with her work colleague. It would be different if she and Felipe were seriously dating—then she'd *have* to tell Eva. But Felipe didn't do serious dating.

Felipe pressed his lips together as if he was holding back on what he wanted to say. 'Of course,' he said finally, standing and pulling her into his arms for a final kiss. 'I've just booked our tickets to Mendoza. Assuming all is well with little Luis, we leave Friday night after work.'

Emilia forced her concerns for Eva to the back of her mind. 'Thank you. I can't wait.'

Except lately, every time she gave herself permission to be excited about being Felipe's date for the wedding, a sense of foreboding rushed in too.

CHAPTER FOURTEEN

THAT SATURDAY FELIPE stood at his brother's side beneath the antique wrought-iron gazebo under an arbour of mature trees on the Castillo Estate. The autumn sun shone as the celebrant pronounced Thiago and Violetta husband and wife, and the bride and groom kissed. Felipe clapped and cheered along with the rest of the congregation, and then breathed a sigh of relief.

The simple ceremony had gone without a hitch. The bride looked stunning, and the pride and love shining in Thiago's eyes had sent a stab of envy through Felipe on more than one occasion throughout the vows.

His stare flicked to Emilia, who was seated with his cousins. Like the rest of the congregation, she too seemed overcome by the romance of the ceremony. She looked breathtaking in her simple emerald-green dress and matching heels, her hair casually pinned up to expose her elegant neck and dangling earrings.

For an unguarded second that niggle of doubt

settled in his gut. Emilia's maternal concern for Eva's welfare was natural, but observing from the outside a part of him worried that, by always putting herself last, Emilia was indefinitely delaying facing up to her own grief. Not that it was any of *his* business. Only if she constantly set her needs aside, where did that leave them? Because his need for *her* grew stronger and more insistent every day. But that was because they had so much in common, he told himself, including a passionate sex life.

Her eyes met his and she smiled. Something inside him reached for her, wished he was at her side, holding her hand. The urge to wrap her in his arms and tell her how beautiful she was, how happy he was that she'd come along as his guest, flared to life. Except his best man duties and their circumstances meant he would need to bide his time.

At Emilia's request, and to avoid the inevitable questions from his family, they were playing this weekend very low key. He'd need to avoid the public displays of affection that now felt like second nature around Emilia to keep up the *just friends* pretence. The last thing either he or Emilia needed was an inquisition from his well-meaning relatives. His aunts in particular considered themselves the family matchmakers, and he didn't want speculation over his and Emilia's relationship to detract from the bride and groom.

'Congratulations,' he said, embracing a delighted Thiago, before he kissed Violetta on both cheeks. 'Mrs Castillo, you look beautiful.'

Violetta laughed, her eyes shining with tears as she turned to hug her bridesmaids. Felipe relaxed for the first time that weekend, the most important part of his best man duties successfully completed: *ensure the groom arrives at the ceremony on time and remember the rings.* As the bride and groom made their way down the aisle, Felipe took his place in the wedding party, escorting the chief bridesmaid, his stare drawn to Emilia.

Reassured that Luis Lopez seemed to be recovering from his latest setback and would avoid a second surgery, they'd arrived at the Castillo Estate late last night. The minute they'd closed the door of the estate's two-bedroomed guest house they'd rushed into each other's arms. Having to keep their relationship secret from people at work and from family was certainly adding to their desperation for each other.

The reception was being held on the two-hundred-year-old bottling barn on the estate, a place of many Castillo family celebrations and countless guest weddings over the years. Having escorted the chief bridesmaid there and temporarily

released from his best man duties, Felipe immediately headed back outside to find Emilia.

Pride filled him as he strode her way. That such
a beautiful, kind and intelligent woman was here
with him made him feel ten feet tall. The weekend
stretched out before them, plenty of time to show
her around the estate, to coax out her wondrous
smile with dancing and good wine, to worship her
body as he'd done late last night and again first
thing this morning. The *one day at a time* plan
seemed to be working out.

She looked up from her phone as he approached,
a small frown pinching her eyebrows together.

'Is everything okay at home, with Eva?' he
asked, pressing a chaste kiss on each of her cheeks
as he'd done to countless relatives that morning,
then offering her his arm. He'd grown attuned to
Emilia's maternal concern, found himself increas-
ingly invested in Eva's well-being in the same the
way he cared about Emilia. And he wanted her to
relax and have a good time today. They worked
hard, they deserved some downtime and a wedding was the perfect occasion.

'I think so,' she said, her voice hesitant. 'She finally replied to my text with an *"I'm fine"*, which
is a little terse for Eva, if I'm honest. Perhaps she's
just a bit lonely. Unless I'm at work, I'm usually
always at home.'

Felipe rested his hand over hers. 'Do you want

to give her a call before the reception? You have plenty of time.' He was dying to introduce Emilia to his extended family and his parents. By the time they'd arrived last night from Mendoza Airport it had been too late for introductions.

Emilia shook her head, pasting on a bright smile. 'No. She'll only accuse me of fussing. I'm sure everything is okay. Let's go have some fun.'

She squeezed his arm and Felipe smiled, wishing he could kiss away that last glimmer of concern in her eyes. He understood the pressures on Emilia. Raising a child wasn't easy, but doing it alone was twice as challenging. Because they'd been getting closer and closer, he knew that Emilia doubted herself as a solo parent, and he wanted to be there for her, but it was fine line to tread without crossing it. He wasn't Eva's father. He didn't know the first thing about raising a child, and he didn't want to get in the way of her close relationship with her mother.

'So, did you enjoy the ceremony?' he asked, changing the subject as they ambled back towards the barn.

'It was so beautiful,' she said, her hand resting on her chest. 'I might have shed an emotional tear or two.'

'Me too,' he said, laughing. 'I'm so proud of my little brother. By the way, you look utterly beautiful. I wanted to tell you earlier but Thiago was a bundle of nerves before the ceremony and wouldn't allow me to leave his side.' He'd almost drooled when he'd spied Emilia taking her seat in the rose garden for the ceremony.

'Thank you.' She smiled. 'You look very smart. And very hot,' she added in a whisper. 'I'm a huge fan of the relaxed wedding attire look,' she said, eyeing his beige linen sports coat and his powder-blue shirt, which was open at the neck.

When her stare returned to his, it carried that secret look he'd now come to expect, the one she gave him when they kissed passionately or when they were intimate, as if she trusted him. He never wanted to lose that trust.

'Are you ready to meet my parents?' Felipe asked as they reached the short line of guests entering the barn, who were being greeted by the bride and groom and both sets of parents. A big part of him wished he could whisk Emilia away somewhere private. It was torture being unable to act naturally, to touch her or kiss her the way he wanted.

'As ready as I'll ever be,' she whispered, giving him a small, nervous smile.

Except Felipe had no doubt that Emilia would charm every single member of his family. If he could keep the intrusive but natural questions about them at bay this weekend it would be a miracle.

Sliding his hand to the small of her back, they entered the barn. 'Mamá, Papá, this is a friend of mine, Emilia Gonzales, a fellow doctor at the General. Emilia, meet Carolina and Gabriel Castillo.'

Pride bloomed in his chest as Emilia greeted his parents warmly, shaking their hands.

'Thank you so much for inviting me,' she said. 'What a beautiful home you have and what a stunning ceremony that was.'

His father beamed and kissed both Emilia's cheeks. His mother's eyes lit up with surprise and predictable speculation as she glanced Felipe's way. He'd have some more explaining to do later, but for now he wasn't ready to answer probing questions about them or put a label on what they had, which was something special but also new and fragile for them both. For now, he simply wanted his beautiful date to forget her worries and have a good time.

They moved away from the line up and headed for the bar. Felipe took two glasses of Castillo Estate bubbles and handed one to Emilia. 'A private toast, just for us,' he said, clinking his glass to hers and enjoying the excited sparkle in her eyes. 'To you, Emilia. To our secret weekend and to family, big or small, here or departed.'

Family was so important to them both, and obviously Ricardo was always in Emilia's thoughts.

He wasn't threatened by that, but he hoped to spend the rest of the weekend making her smile.

Emilia swallowed, blinking up at him, her emotions clearly on display. 'That's a beautiful toast, Felipe. To family,' she replied, her eyes sad but hopeful.

They took a first sip, their stares locked together. The rest of the room seemed to fade out, as if they were alone. Felipe stiffened, restless. How would he get through today without holding her the way he wanted to, without kissing her and showing everyone here how passionately he wanted this incredible woman, who had also become a great friend?

Her stare shifted over his face, as if she too felt the same impulses. Then she blinked and the moment passed. 'I hope you're keeping some of that good stuff for your best man toast.'

Felipe grinned, recalling how he'd promised to play down their connection—he'd need to stop looking at her as if he couldn't wait to strip off that dress. 'I'll try to pull something out of the hat.'

Emilia took another sip of wine and glanced around the crowded room, where the party was already in full swing, the music playing, the drinks flowing, joy and laughter a loud din. 'Do you know everyone here?' she asked.

Felipe shrugged, stepping closer because she

felt too far away. 'My father is one of five brothers.' He indicated the huddle of uncles in the far corner, drinking and laughing and generally staying away from their wives—his aunts—probably in case they were tasked with some job or other.

'I have fifteen cousins,' he added. 'I'll introduce you to a few more, but don't worry—you don't have to remember everyone's names.'

Emilia smiled, looking relieved. 'And all the children are little Castillos?'

'The children of my cousins,' Felipe confirmed. 'Oh, I forgot. Speaking of children, I wanted to show you something. Come with me.'

He guided her out of the rear door of the barn, taking her hand as they crossed a cobblestoned courtyard, which later would be lit with a thousand twinkling lights as dusk settled.

'This is it,' Felipe said, pausing at the foot of a set of stone steps, where a huge concrete planter spilled over with flowers. 'This is my vat, where I trod my first vintage.'

Emilia's eyes lit up.

'See,' he said, running his finger over the brass plate engraved with his name and a date. 'I was six years old. Come—I'll show you.'

He opened the door to another barn used for storage and office space, locating the framed photograph on the wall. 'That's me.' He was treading

the grapes for the first time and was so small that
he barely reached over the side of the vat.

Emilia peered closer, her smile full of wonder.
'Oh, you were an adorable little boy. And look
at that cheeky smile.' She beamed up at him and
he slipped his arm around her waist, pulling her
close because they were alone.

'It's the same as this one,' he said, smiling
down at her. 'I haven't been able to wipe it off
my face today, because you're here.' He brushed
her lips with his, tasting lipstick and wine and
Emilia. 'Thank you for coming. I know my big
noisy family are a bit overwhelming. But say the
word and we'll duck out for a break. I know all
the best hiding places around here.'

'I'll remember that,' she said breathily, her stare
dipping to his mouth so he once more captured
her lips in a kiss.

Fire raced through his blood and their kiss
turned passionate. Emilia slid her arm around
his waist, inside his jacket, as she parted her lips
and touched her tongue to his. Felipe forgot where
he was, forgot that as far as anyone else here was
concerned, they were *just friends*, forgot that he'd
spent fifteen years keeping the women he dated
at arm's length.

Emilia was different. She was special. He
wanted her too much to keep a lid on his feelings,
even though they were terrifying. But as long as

he kept them to himself, as long as he didn't pressure her to consider them dating exclusively for a while, he could examine them more closely after this weekend.

'Felipe…' she moaned as he pressed kisses down the side on her neck, hitting all the spots that made her gasp when he moved inside her. His hand roamed the body he now knew so well, cupping her breast, her waist, her hip and her backside as her fingers slid through his hair, bringing him back to their kiss.

They were like a flame and oxygen—one touch, one look, one word setting off a chain reaction of desire until they surrendered and quenched it in each other's arms. Emilia pressed her body to his, moving against him so he grew painfully hard, his only thought to wonder if they had time to slip back to the guest house.

'I can't wait to get you alone later,' he whispered against her lips, his hand fisting the fabric of her dress over her hip. 'I'm going to peel off this beautiful dress, cover your body in kisses, spend the whole night pleasuring you, making you come so many times you won't ever forget this weekend.'

Emilia licked her lips, her eyes glazed over with passion and she gripped the lapel of his jacket as if for balance. 'I can't wait. But we should get

back. You're the best man. They'll start looking
for you soon.'

'Party pooper,' he teased, pressing one last
chaste kiss to her smiling lips.

'I'll make it up to you later,' she said seduc-
tively, batting her long eyelashes so he almost
groaned.

Felipe stepped back and reached for her hand.
'I guess I can keep my hands off you for a few
hours longer. Come on, let's introduce you to even
more people.'

It promised to be a wonderful party, but for Felipe it would also be a very long day.

CHAPTER FIFTEEN

As DARKNESS FELL the sultry beat of the tango music began, the band striking up the famous intro to *La Cumparista* which, while linked with Buenos Aires, had originated in Emilia's native Uruguay.

On the dance floor, Emilia smiled as Felipe drew her close into his arms, their bodies scandalously close. Her heart, already skipping from dancing all night long, fluttered to new heights as they moved provocatively around the dance floor. Felipe was a great dancer.

Emilia breathed in the scent of his warm body and his spicy cologne, the memory of that searing kiss in the barn making her bones melt. Romantic, seductive Felipe was dangerous, and she had a hard enough time resisting regular Felipe. But in a couple more hours they could retreat to the guest house and finally be alone.

Smiling up at him, she released a contented sigh. Everything about today—the wedding, the reception, the dancing—had been magical.

Maybe it was how hot he looked, or the delicious wine that had flowed all day, or the excessive romance of both the location and occasion, but Felipe had made Emilia feel beautiful and cherished. It had been a long time since she'd been so joyous and content.

Was it wrong that she'd only thought about Ricardo a handful of times today? She would always love him deeply, but being here with Felipe, having such a fun time, it was as if she'd finally given herself permission to find new ways to be happy.

She dragged in a breath, her head swimming with fear that such feelings couldn't possibly be trusted. The last time she'd felt happy and content, Ricardo had fallen sick. Could the universe be cruel enough to steal this feeling from her a second time? And was she wrong to associate happiness with a man who was all about having a good time, but when it came to feelings never thought about tomorrow?

Because she didn't want to tempt fate, she cleared the doubts from her head with a shake and leaned back to look at Felipe. 'Are you having a good time now that your best man duties are behind you?' she asked, intentionally spoiling the moment of intense intimacy created by the dance.

His entire family were watching. They couldn't perform the tango, the most seductive dance on the planet, as freely and naturally as they wanted to. If they did, everyone would know they were sleeping together. Their pretence of *just friends* would be exposed. And if they weren't friends, what were they? What did she even want them to be?

Felipe stared down at her, his feet gliding over the floor, carrying her along. 'I'm having a wonderful time, and it's all down to you.' His stare lingered on her lips and she held her breath. Would he kiss her in front of everyone? 'Thank you for being my date,' he said instead, perhaps sensing her withdrawal.

Emilia's cheeks heated at his caution when there was stark passion in Felipe's eyes. But he was a passionate man. Combined with the way he was holding her, as if he'd never let her go, she was having a hard time remembering that they weren't alone, not to mention that he deliberately kept his passion superficial.

'Thank you for inviting me,' she said, grateful. 'I've had a lovely day. Your family is as charming as you are. They've all made me feel so welcome.' She couldn't recall the last time she'd enjoyed herself so much or felt so light-hearted.

He shrugged and smiled. 'That's the Castillo way. Perhaps next time we visit we could also bring Eva. There are plenty of my cousins' children her age.'

Emilia nodded vaguely, her pulse flying. What

was happening here? Return visits, bringing Eva along, the way they'd made love late last night and again early this morning, as if reaching for each other had become second nature.

Before she could examine the terrified lurch of her heart, Felipe said, 'My parents loved you by the way. They dragged me aside earlier and asked if we're more than friends.'

Emilia scoffed, that carefree part of her that he'd brought back to life desperate to know if they could ever be more, and the rest of her rejecting the idea flat out. She still loved *Ricardo*. There was no room in her heart for Felipe. Except since she'd first met him a few short weeks ago she'd changed, grown somehow, learned new things about herself and found fresh resilience.

She'd spent so many years putting herself and her needs last out of necessity. Two parents raising a child while holding down full-time jobs was hard enough. Raising a grieving child solo, while also grieving herself, had put Emilia into survival mode. But the past few weeks had shown her that she wanted more for her future. She didn't want to be alone as Eva built her own life. She would always be there for her daughter, but she also wanted things for herself. To enjoy the good things in life, to laugh in good company and maybe even to love again one day.

Immediately dismissing the possibility, she

shuddered. It was probably just a romance hangover from the wedding.

'Don't worry,' Felipe said, reading into her pensive silence. 'I told them to relax. They'll be the first to know if I ever decide to once more embark on another serious relationship.'

Emilia pulled a watery smile. It didn't matter how much *she'd* grown. Felipe, the only man she'd met recently who she could see herself in a relationship with, was a staunch commitment-phobe who'd been single for fifteen years. She needed to remember that he might be a passionate lover and a considerate friend and colleague, but he clearly wasn't thinking about them having any sort of lasting relationship. If she wasn't careful, if she didn't hold back and protect herself while this fling ran its course, she could get badly hurt.

'By the way,' he asked, 'did you hear back from Eva?'

Emilia had texted earlier, checking in that all was well back at home. She shook her head, fingers of concern creeping up her spine now that he'd reminded her. 'No, she must be busy. She said she might go to social volleyball, so perhaps she's hanging out with friends.'

Felipe nodded and the song came to an end. Emilia stepped out of his close embrace, her head all over the place, as if the spell of the wedding and that feeling of contentment had been broken.

'I think I'll get a glass of water,' she said. 'All this dancing has made me thirsty.'

'I'll get it for you,' he offered. 'Why don't you sit at our table and I'll bring it over?'

Emilia returned to their table, gratefully sank into a chair and kicked off her heels to ease her aching feet. She hadn't danced so much in years. But now that the seed of doubt had germinated, she wondered if she was making a fool of herself with him, just like those other women he dated who saw his wonderful attentiveness as a sign of commitment he just wasn't into, or maybe even capable of given his regrets over his marriage. As she watched Felipe at the bar, she probed her feelings, tasting fear. Was she already falling for Felipe Castillo?

Just then someone sat beside her. 'Are you having fun, dear?' the elderly woman asked.

She was one of Felipe's aunts, but Emilia couldn't for the life of her recall her name.

'Yes, I am. What a beautiful wedding and a great party.' Emilia smiled broadly. 'I'm sorry. I've forgotten your name.' She'd drunk too much wine and met too many people to risk getting it wrong.

'I'm Lucia,' the other woman said with a smile, 'Felipe's oldest and favourite aunt.' She winked playfully. 'So you and Felipe work in the same field at the hospital?'

Emilia nodded, happy to talk about her work rather than analyse her jumbled and scary feelings. 'Yes, we're both neonatal surgeons, although Felipe is senior to me. He's been mentoring me while I get my Argentinian practising certificate.'

'How smart you are,' Lucia said, impressed. 'And my nephew tells me that you have a lovely daughter.'

'Eva,' Emilia said, wondering again if Eva was okay at home alone. 'She's eighteen and has just started law at university.'

'Ah…clever, like her mother. My grandson is eighteen. That's him on the dance floor, the tall one.'

'He's very handsome,' Emilia said.

'That's Castillo men, for you.' Lucia's shrewd eyes filled with mischief. 'But I don't need to tell *you* that. You and Felipe make a very attractive couple.'

Emilia flushed from head to toe—she'd known the tango was a mistake. 'Oh, no…we're not together. We're…just friends.' Only a part of her— that secret, locked away part that was scared to open her heart to love—had maybe foolishly started to imagine them as more.

Lucia shooed away Emilia's lame explanation. 'Oh, nonsense,' she said with all the authority of a veteran matchmaker. 'The family aren't fooled. Felipe's clearly in love with you. And about time too. He deserves to find happiness again. And if the way you look at him is any indication, you're in love with him too.'

Emilia froze, her blood running cold. 'In love…?'

No, no, no… She couldn't be in love with Felipe.

'Yes, love,' Lucia said, oblivious to the fear and turmoil flooding Emilia's entire body. 'The other aunts think we might soon have another wedding at Castillo Estates.' The older woman winked suggestively.

Emilia lips twitched automatically, although she'd never felt less like smiling. Her blood rushed with panic. She sought out Felipe who'd been waylaid on his way back from the bar by a group of male relatives. He glanced her way and their eyes met, locked—his were smiling.

With her stomach twisted into knots, Emilia looked away quickly, confused by what she saw in his expression and by the painful turmoil in her chest. Could it be true that he had feelings for her? No, Felipe's aunts must be mistaken. Felipe didn't want a serious relationship, he'd literally *just* told her that on the dance floor. And as for her…had she missed the signs? Did her feelings for Felipe go beyond respect, friendship and passion? Was that why their relationship, their growing closeness, seemed less like a betrayal of Ricardo and more and more natural? No, she couldn't forget her husband so easily. She would hate herself if that happened and Eva would never forgive her.

'But maybe I'm getting ahead of myself,' Lucia admitted sheepishly, patting Emilia's arm affectionately. 'Don't listen to me, dear. I'm an old romantic at heart.'

Emilia tried to smile, except the damage was already done. The floodgates had opened and Emilia was swamped by her feelings. Overwhelmed.

Just then a small huddle of children rushed over and interrupted. 'Abuela, Abuela…' they called, dragging off their grandmother.

Shaking inside, Emilia slipped on her shoes and headed for the bathroom. She wasn't ready for an emotional realisation. Not now, not with all these people watching her and secretly commenting. She needed a moment to herself to process that conversation and what it had unearthed, away from prying eyes and more importantly away from Felipe. If she had fallen for him, she couldn't tell him. Unless her feelings were already obvious to him? Was that why he'd made his point about avoiding serious relationships on the dance floor? To warn her off?

Ducking into the bathroom, she locked herself in a cubicle and leaned back against the cool wood of the closed door, her heart thudding wildly. Her head was all over the place, but she tried to think rationally. Her fear and panic every time she thought about having more than what they had now was understandable. If she thought seriously about her own needs, about moving on, about opening her heart up to another man and falling in love again, it felt like a betrayal of Ricardo and everything they'd had for over twenty years.

But she *did* have feelings for Felipe. How could she not? He was a great man—caring and compassionate and romantic. That didn't make it *love*. Was she even capable of love again, after losing her beloved husband? She'd grown so used to shoving down her own feelings and concentrating on Eva that now she wasn't sure which way was up.

She didn't want to embarrass herself by putting herself out there and telling him how she felt. She'd only be risking further heartache if Felipe didn't feel the same way. And what did all this mean for Eva? Emilia didn't want her relationship with Felipe to hurt or upset her daughter in any way. Eva would always be her main priority.

Pulling her phone from her purse, Emilia checked for a reply to the text she'd sent to her daughter earlier.

I'm okay. Feeling a little sad for some reason. Talk tomorrow. Eva xx.

A chill of foreboding raised goosebumps over her bare arms. How could she have become so carried away enjoying herself that she'd neglected to check in with her daughter? What if Eva wasn't *okay*? And why was she feeling sad?

Emilia dialled Eva's number but the call went straight to voicemail. It was past eleven-thirty— maybe she was already asleep. Or maybe she *was* upset, while Emilia had been dancing and putting her own irrelevant feelings first. She was a mother, a mature woman. Why was she hiding in the toilets, agonising over her feelings for a man who might never return them?

Ashamed of herself, Emilia left the cubicle and washed her hands. Coming to the wedding had been a mistake. She'd put her own needs first and made a fool of herself, acted like a love-struck teenager in front of Felipe's family.

With her temples throbbing and her insides a trembling mess, she headed back to the party to find Felipe.

CHAPTER SIXTEEN

By the time Felipe wound up his conversation with his cousin Mateo, Emilia seemed to have disappeared. Felipe scanned the barn, a vague rumble of unease in his gut. Then he came face to face with Thiago.

'My best man—are you enjoying yourself?' Thiago asked jovially, slinging his arm around Felipe's shoulders.

'Absolutely,' Felipe replied, his smile for his brother genuine. 'It's been a great day. But more importantly, are *you* happy?'

Thiago released Felipe and spread his arms wide. 'I'm a married man. Of course I'm happy.'

Felipe laughed, thinking back to his own wedding day, so many years ago. He'd been so young, full of optimism and confidence that his marriage to Delfina would work out. But somehow, as the years had passed, they'd grown in opposite directions, and Felipe had lived with the consequences ever since. Felipe prayed for his brother's sake that Thiago and Violetta would last the distance. At least Thiago had maturity on his side, and a partner who seemed to share his dreams and goals as much as he shared hers.

'Everyone loves Emilia,' Thiago continued. 'She's a real hit.' He slapped his brother's back. 'Nice work.'

'Thanks.' Felipe laughed good-naturedly, his stare seeking her out once more. If he'd been on the marriage market, Emilia would indeed be a very good catch. They shared so much—their world views, their careers, their personal aspirations. Not to mention intense physical passion. The more time he spent with her the closer he felt to her. It was no surprise to him that Emilia was the reason he currently felt so…content.

'So what's the plan?' Thiago asked. 'Are you two still casual? Please tell me you're not going to watch her date any more idiots? Maybe you should think about popping the question.'

Felipe laughed nervously, prickles of unease creeping up his neck. His family meant well, but he could sense the pressure building. Emilia had stiffened in his arms earlier when he'd mentioned his parents' questions. And she obviously had a lot on her mind with Eva. The last thing he wanted to do was transmit any of that pressure to Emilia and scare her off.

'Listen,' he said, turning serious, 'things are… delicate between us. We're not in our twenties.

We both have our pasts to deal with and Emilia's daughter is her priority, quite rightly.' Felipe winced. 'Please don't say anything to scare her off. I really like her.'

Thiago was right in one thing. Felipe didn't want to watch Emilia go on any more dates. *He* wanted to be her date. He wanted more than just great sex and friendship. But his family were unaware of the fine details of his relationship with Emilia. He didn't want one of them to inadvertently put their foot in it or spook her. And as his feelings for her deepened there was already enough pressure within himself to ask her where their relationship was headed.

After fifteen years of staying single, he couldn't simply rush in and make her any promises. Maybe they could continue to build on their connection, one day at a time. Maybe he should ask her to be exclusive but take things slowly.

'Of course,' Thiago said, resting his hand over his heart. 'You have my word. I understand how it's more complicated second time around. But if you really like her...'

Thiago's voice drifted off as he peered over Felipe's shoulder, his eyes widening. 'Here she comes.' He embraced Felipe, spoke briefly to Emilia, kissed her cheek and wandered off.

'There you are,' Felipe said with smile, handing over her glass of water. She looked pale and distracted. 'Are you okay?' he asked, alarmed.

Had she overheard any of his conversation with Thiago? Felipe had no idea how Emilia felt about them having something more than casual sex, and she was obviously still grieving for Ricardo. But perhaps they could enjoy each other's company while it lasted. Suddenly, the idea felt hollow, as if he already knew it wouldn't be enough for him.

When she said nothing, placing her drink on a nearby table without touching it, Felipe's alarm grew. Had she received bad news? 'Is it Eva?' He ran his hands down her bare arms, chasing away her goosebumps. 'Is everything okay at home?'

'I'm not sure...' She shivered, dragging in a deep breath, but she couldn't quite meet his eye. 'I don't think it's anything serious, but she said she's feeling a bit sad and now she's no longer answering my texts.'

Felipe's mind reeled. Of course she'd be distracted by concern for Eva while being so far away. He was a little worried, too.

'Have you called the house?' he asked, snagging his jacket from the chair and draping it over her shoulders to ward off the chill.

She shook her head vaguely. 'No... But I tried her cell phone.' She raised her hand to her temple. 'I... I'm sorry. I'm not feeling that well. I have a headache, suddenly. Probably stress. I might call it a night if that's okay.'

A swell of compassion engulfed him. He wrapped his arm around her and held her close. 'Of course it's okay,' he said. 'Let's get you some painkillers. I'll walk you back to the guest house.'

'Oh, no…' Emilia pulled back, her stare flitting everywhere but at him. 'Please don't interrupt your evening on my account. It's your brother's wedding.'

He winced at his automatic display of affection. Of course Emilia wanted their relationship to remain a secret, but he couldn't help his feelings. He cared deeply about this woman. It was second nature to touch her and comfort her, to try and be there for her.

'Emilia, it's no problem,' he said in a low voice, trying to be discreet. 'Let me look after you. I can run you a bath if that will help with the headache.'

She shook her head, a determined tilt to her chin. 'Actually, I think I might go back to Buenos Aires on the first flight tomorrow morning.'

Stunned, Felipe all but gaped. 'Is that really necessary? I'm sure Eva is fine. I had plans to show you the estate tomorrow.' Her concern for her daughter was understandable, but taking an early flight home seemed like a bit of an overreaction. Unless there was something else going on…

'If I don't go,' she continued, 'I'll just spend the

rest of the weekend worrying. And I don't want to make a fuss or be a bother to your family at this happy time.' Her stare flicked around the room, where the other guests were still in high spirits, then she looked at him, imploring.

'Of course...' His mind scrambled to catch up. Had he upset her in some way? 'Why don't you get some rest?' he urged. 'I'll change our flights to the morning.'

She shook her head, already backing away, as if she feared he might try to hold onto her. 'No, I don't want to interrupt your weekend celebration with your family, and you're the best man. I've already called a taxi to take me to a hotel near the airport for tonight, so I don't disturb anyone when I leave early. Can you please thank your parents from me and wish the bride and groom farewell? I'll just quietly slip out now.'

That was when he spied her overnight bag at her feet, his stomach sinking. She'd already been back to the guest house and collected her things. There was clearly no persuading her to stay. Confusion settled like a weight in his chest. What was happening? Had he inadvertently moved too fast? Spooked her? They'd been having a great time, and now it seemed she couldn't wait to get away from him.

Her phone pinged with a text and she shrugged

off his jacket, handing it over. 'I'm sorry Felipe. I really have to go. My taxi is almost here.'

'I'll walk you out,' he said, feeling numb and a little stupid, as if he'd done something wrong but had no idea what. 'Will you call me, when you get to the hotel?' he asked, reaching for her hand as they walked towards the estate's gate at the top of the driveway.

'Okay,' she said, her voice devoid of any warmth.

'And if you hear from Eva. I'm concerned, too.' How could he enjoy the rest of the party with everything between them up in the air? Couldn't she understand that he cared about her and her daughter?

A hundred questions stuck in his throat at the sudden change in Emilia. He'd thought they were growing closer, but now he was filled with doubts. Maybe he'd misjudged things. Maybe she was still grieving too much for a new relationship, even a casual one. Maybe she still wasn't ready to put her own needs first.

'Listen,' he said as they paused at the top of the drive. 'I understand that you must put Eva first, but I want you to know that I loved every minute of you being here with me this weekend. It's made me realise that we might be able to have something more than just a casual fling.'

She opened her mouth to speak but he held up his hand. 'No pressure, nothing serious, but maybe we could be exclusive, only dating each other. That way you wouldn't have to experience any more bad dates, and I wouldn't have to worry about clingy women looking for a proposal.' He tried to smile, but it felt like his face was made of rubber and Emilia looked horrified. As he'd talked, her eyes had widened, as if with growing fear, and a pulse ticked frantically in her neck. Not the reaction he'd hoped for.

'You don't have to answer now,' he added, deflated. 'Just have a think about it.' Felipe sucked in some breaths, feeling as if he'd just run a marathon and then ripped his racing heart out of his chest and held it out to her as a gift. How had he misjudged this so badly?

She gripped both his hands, looking up at him and held his stare. 'I've really enjoyed getting to know you, and this weekend has been wonderful, the most fun I've had in years.' She paused, looked down at her feet, and Felipe heard the *but* coming as if from a mile away. His stomach sank.

She looked up, smiled sadly. 'You've helped me to move past my grief, and I'll always be grateful to you for that.'

Internally, Felipe recoiled. He didn't want her gratitude. He wanted her passion. He knew it was there—he felt it every time they touched. But maybe she was holding out for more. Maybe when her heart had healed she'd go searching for someone she could love again. Someone without his track record for failing when it came to relationships. Someone who could be her *Mr Right*.

'But we agreed to keep it casual,' she went on, calmly delivering the final blow. 'I'm still finding my way as a single parent, still acclimatising to a new job and a new country. Still figuring out if I want to even be in another relationship in the future. I don't think I can devote energy to anything else right now.'

Felipe stiffened. This sounded like goodbye, not just from the weekend but from *them*. He glanced away and saw distant headlights slowly approaching in the dark. Emilia's taxi.

'So you don't want to see me again? Not even casually?' he asked, his throat raw. How could she just walk away after everything they'd shared? How could he let her go when it felt so utterly wrong? But he couldn't force her to care about him or want to date him. Maybe she was right. Maybe he'd never be what she needed. Maybe to try and cling onto something with her would only hurt her, and by extension Eva, in the long run.

'I can't risk having feelings for you, Felipe.' She tilted her head and squeezed his hand, but he was in no way comforted. She saw through him, saw how he might let her down. 'Maybe it's best to call it a day now,' she went on, 'before we both get our hearts broken. Neither of us needs that.'

Felipe nodded, his mind and body reeling. She was right to protect herself. The last time he'd tried a serious relationship he'd been a bad husband, and he'd spent years since then swearing off commitment. But now that she was ending it, now that there was a hole blown through the centre of his chest, he could clearly see that it was already too late for him. He already had deep, deep feelings for Emilia. Not that it was enough.

The taxi pulled up. Emilia pressed a brief kiss to his cheek, her soft and warm lips doing nothing to ward off the chill in his bones. 'Thank you for a lovely weekend. I'll always remember it.'

He frowned, silently watching her walk away. She handed her overnight bag to the driver and quickly ducked into the back seat without a backward glance. Felipe stood frozen, rocked to the core. Just like that, what had begun so passionately and unexpectedly was over.

As the taxi drove away—the taillights getting smaller and smaller, finally disappearing around a bend in the road—Felipe could only reel in shock and pain. It was a weekend he'd never forget either, a weekend he'd always remember as the time he had his wise old heart crushed to smithereens.

CHAPTER SEVENTEEN

THE TRIP HOME to Buenos Aires without Felipe had taken a lifetime, beginning with the endless taxi ride down Castillo Estate's driveway. Emilia had forced herself to look straight ahead, rather than turn around to see if Felipe had watched her leave or simply headed back to the party. After a few sleepless hours in the airport hotel, the two-hour flight home had only provided her with more time to think and feel and tie herself into knots over the decisions she'd made.

She'd run scared, there was no dressing it up. But now she needed to own her choice, because it had been the right one.

Regardless of her feelings for him, Felipe's matchmaking aunts had been wrong. He wasn't in love with her. Of course he'd enjoyed the good time they'd had together, enjoyed the sex, but the only thing he'd wanted was for them to date exclusively.

And for Emilia, with so much on the line— *her* happiness, Eva's happiness, even her job—

his underwhelming offer was too great a risk to her fragile heart.

Numbly opening the front door, Emilia dumped her bag in the hall. She poked her head inside Eva's room, finding her daughter safe and asleep, before stooping to greet Luna and letting her out into the garden.

Emilia shuffled into the kitchen and reached for the coffee, glancing at the clock. Ten a.m. Thank goodness it was Sunday. She had another twenty-four hours before she had to face Felipe at work. How would they act with each other now that they were returning to being just work colleagues? Would there be awkwardness, bad feelings, regret? Could they still be friends when she'd obviously confused him and hurt his feelings?

No, they were mature adults. They'd manage their working relationship as they always had: with mutual respect and collaboration. Except no matter how much she tried to convince herself that all would be well, Emilia couldn't seem to shake the terrible feeling in the pit of her stomach that she'd done something terribly wrong.

'You're back,' Eva said sleepily, coming into the room still wearing her pyjamas. 'I thought your flight was this evening.' She stepped automatically into her mother's embrace and Emilia held her too tight for too long.

'Good morning, *mija*.' She pasted on a bright

smile as Eva stepped back. 'I came home early. I have some admin to catch up on.'

'That sounds dull.' Eva frowned, reaching for the kettle to make herself some tea. 'So how was the wedding?'

Emilia's breath caught—*confusing, painful, one big mistake.*

'It was lovely,' she said, her stomach taking another sickening dive. If she kept talking, she wouldn't have time to reflect on the look of disappointment and hurt on Felipe's face when she'd told him they were done. 'Very romantic and such a stunning location.' Emilia took a sip of coffee, her eyes stinging at the way the weekend had ended. 'But it's good to be home.'

Yes, *home* was where her focus needed to be. Away from Felipe she could gain some perspective. And surely, with a good night's sleep behind her, she'd soon see that her choice to end things was for the best. She couldn't go on being heartbroken at her age. Only her chest ached every time she thought of him and what she'd done. His pain and confusion had been so difficult to witness.

'Mamá, you weren't even gone forty-eight hours,' Eva scolded.

'Never mind about that,' Emilia said, shoving her own feelings aside. 'How are *you*? Do you still feel sad? I was a little worried when I saw your text last night.'

Eva gasped, turning to face her mother. 'You didn't come home early for *me*, did you?'

'Not really...' Emilia waved her hand dismissively as she sipped her coffee, downplaying her concern. 'I mean of course I was concerned. You seemed very distracted when I left Friday, and then you said you were feeling sad, and then you stopped answering my texts...'

'Only because I fell *asleep*,' Eva explained, her eyes wide and shining with tears. 'I'm sorry if I ruined your weekend.'

'Don't be silly, mija. You didn't ruin anything.' She drew Eva into another hug, uncertain which of them needed it the most. 'Are you sad because of Papá?' Emilia whispered into her daughter's hair.

Eva nodded, her face crumpling. 'The truth is,' she said with a sniff, 'that I *have* been struggling these past couple of weeks.'

Emilia nodded for her to continue, brushing away Eva's tears. 'That's okay. I'm always here for you, you know that.'

Eva blinked, looking uncertain. 'It's just that everything is new. Everything seems to be changing so fast.' She winced, crossing her arms over her waist defensively. '*I* was the one who encouraged you to date, but then when you did I pan-

icked, because I suddenly thought about Papá.'
She raised tear-reddened eyes to Emilia and whispered, 'What if we forget him? I never want that
to happen.'

'Oh, Eva,' Emilia cried, cupping her daughter's
face so she couldn't hide her emotions from her
mother. 'We'll *never* forget him. Never. He'll always be in our hearts.'

Emilia wiped the tears from her daughter's
cheeks, the way she had when Eva had been a
little girl, feeling choked herself. 'I see him every
time I look at you,' she continued. 'I feel him
smiling when you do something that makes me
proud, I even talk to him in my head about how
well you're doing at uni and the new friends
you've made.'

Eva nodded uncertainly.

'Come on.' Emilia grabbed their drinks and
they sat on the sofa. She turned to Eva. 'I know
we've been through some big changes recently,
but now that we're settled here in Buenos Aires
nothing else is going to change, I promise.'

Of course Eva felt overwhelmed after everything she'd been through.

'My full registration with the Argentine Medical Council is almost through,' Emilia said, 'so
my job is secure, and I've decided that I'm not dating any more, so there'll be no more distractions.
In fact, I came home early from Mendoza because

I ended things with Felipe last night. From now on my focus is back where it should be, on you and me and building our new life.'

'No, Mamá,' Eva said, horrified, fresh tears spilling over her lids. 'Why did you do that? Felipe makes you so happy.'

'I…' Emilia trailed off, lost for words. She had no idea Eva had intuited so much about her relationship with Felipe. But it was too late now. She'd made her decision and the damage was done. She shook her head. 'It doesn't matter how he makes me feel. *You* are my priority. I've had my chance at happiness with your father, that's why I won't ever forget him. I'm happy to be alone, really I am.'

Eva gripped Emilia's hands. 'No… I've seen you smile more since you met Felipe. You deserve to be *truly* happy, not just going through the motions.'

'I *am* happy.' She smiled, but the expression felt unconvincing.

'But I don't want you be alone because of me,' Eva insisted. 'I'm just taking a little longer than anticipated to adjust, that's all.'

Emilia nodded. 'I understand. I'm struggling to adjust too.' She dragged in a shuddering breath, laying herself open and being completely honest with her daughter, who wasn't a child any more and deserved the truth. 'But you're right,' she said.

'I *have* felt lighter and happier since meeting Felipe. Only I'm not sure I'm ready to fall in love again. It's terrifying.'

Eva reached for her hand, her gaze sympathetic.

'What if it doesn't work out?' Emilia continued. 'What if my relationship with Felipe hurts you? What if I *do* fall in love with him and I lose him too?'

At that final question, her own eyes stung with tears, and she hung her head. This was the deepest root of her fear. She was scared to make herself vulnerable again, fully open to love, because of the pain she'd experienced from loving and losing Ricardo. She'd never survive it a second time.

'I know nothing will bring him back,' Eva said in a hushed whisper, 'but if you could do it all again with Papá, knowing what was to come, would you?'

'Of course,' Emilia said without hesitation, her own tears spilling freely down her cheeks. How was her eighteen-year-old so emotionally intelligent? So wise when Emilia had been so foolish as to run scared?

'Because loving him all over again would be worth the risk,' Eva said. Emilia nodded.

'Worth *any* risk,' Emilia confirmed, realising now how she'd been standing in her own way of experiencing happiness again. Loving someone carried massive risks, yes, but also even greater rewards.

'So if Felipe makes you so happy,' Eva urged, 'after everything we've been through, all the sadness and loss and change, don't you think you owe it to yourself to see where your relationship with him could go, regardless of the risks? What if you *do* fall in love again? Wouldn't it be worth it, the way it was with Papá?'

'Maybe,' Emilia said in a choked voice, ashamed of herself. 'I just got scared,' she admitted, 'at the wedding.'

Her daughter squeezed her hand. 'I can understand why,' Eva said. 'I'm scared too, because change is hard, and when Papá was well our lives were so wonderful.'

'Yes, they were.' Emilia nodded, her heart clenching with love for Eva. As a little family, they'd had it all. But could she have it all again?

'I love Papá and I'll always miss him,' Eva said, 'but I think it's time that we let him go a little and start over properly with open hearts. We both need to be brave and embrace all the new changes in our lives. Don't you think?'

'You're right.' Emilia sniffed, taking a tissue from the box on the coffee table. Could she set aside her fear of losing someone she loved and open her heart fully?

Eva was right. If she found love it would be

worth any risk. To have someone who understood you, cherished and supported you, and you them in return—it was rare and precious. And she was falling in love with Felipe.

'But you're already so brave,' Emilia said, sniffling into a wad of tissues. 'Whereas I wasn't brave. One of Felipe's aunts said something to me at the wedding, how she thought Felipe and I looked like we were in love and it spooked me. So I allowed my fear to make my decisions and I ran away.'

She had cut Felipe off without giving him a chance because she was scared to open her heart fully to him. Scared that, because of their pasts, any serious relationship between them would be doomed to failure and she'd be hurt again. Scared to love and to lose.

Eva frowned. 'Maybe he *does* love you. But that's a good thing, isn't it?'

Emilia shrugged, her heart sore. 'If it's true, it's good. Because I think the aunt might be right about me. I *have* fallen in love with him, the way I fell for Papá. But would that upset you?'

Eva smiled, fresh tears glittering on her long dark lashes. 'You never needed my permission to move on, Mamá. I want you to be happy. But I think you need to tell Felipe that you love him. It's the brave thing to do, and he deserves to know.'

Emilia dragged in a breath and nodded. 'You're

right. He does.' Even if he didn't love her in return. 'I'll tell him first thing tomorrow morning.'

She didn't want to tell him something so important by text, and he would be leaving Mendoza soon for the afternoon flight they'd been supposed to take together.

As she held her daughter until the tears dried, Emilia silently spoke to Ricardo. *I'm so proud of our girl.'*

She would always love him, always prioritise Eva in her life, but it was time for Emilia to finally put her own needs first. It was time to be brave. It was time to love again.

CHAPTER EIGHTEEN

LATER THAT SUNDAY evening Felipe emerged into the domestic terminal of Buenos Aires airport after his flight from Mendoza, his frustration and impatience an itch under his skin.

The flight home had seemed endless.

He checked his watch. Seven-thirty p.m. Not too late to call Emilia. She'd probably be at home, alone or perhaps with Eva. She'd texted him earlier today to let him know that all was well. But it wasn't, not with him. His stomach lurched with fear. He should never have let her leave.

Turning to Thiago and Violetta behind him, he dropped his overnight bag and held open his arms. 'Well, have a wonderful honeymoon, you two.' He kissed Violetta on the cheek and hugged Thiago, pasting on a fake smile.

The couple had been on the same flight from Mendoza—the one Emilia and he were supposed to take together before she'd run out on him Saturday night. The newlyweds were heading to the international terminal to take their connecting flight to the Caribbean island of Aruba for two weeks.

'We will,' Violetta said, stepping back, but Thiago hesitated.

'Darling,' his brother said to his new wife, 'could you give me a second? I just need some brotherly advice.'

'Of course.' Violetta smiled encouragingly at both men and ambled a short distance away to give them privacy.

'What's up,' Felipe asked, impatient to be on his way. Maybe he'd forget calling and simply knock on Emilia's door. He had to do something to make things right before he lost his mind, because the last time they'd spoken his words had come out wrong, his feelings tripping him up. He needed to make her want him again. 'I hope you're not going to ask me what to expect on your honeymoon, because you're a little old for the birds and bees talk.'

His joke masked the painful hollow feeling in his chest. All he'd wanted to do since he'd watched Emilia drive away was chase her down and beg her to reconsider. It had taken her leaving him stranded in the dark to realise that he'd fallen madly in love with her, and he had no idea what to do about it. But missing her was a physical pain all over his body. He needed to see her, to beg her to give him another chance.

'I was going to ask *you* what's up, actually,' Thiago said, ignoring Felipe's attempt at humour. 'You haven't really been present since Emilia left last night. I know you tried to convince everyone that you two are *just friends*, but it's time to be real.' Thiago tilted his head sympathetically. 'Especially because you're acting as if she cut out your heart when she left.'

Felipe gripped the back of his neck and exhaled noisily. He was fifty-five years old. He didn't need love-life advice from his little brother. Except maybe he did. Because Thiago was right. His heart had been ripped out. Maybe he should hear his brother out, seeing as on his own he'd made such a mess of his relationship with Emilia.

'If you must know,' Felipe said with a sigh, 'we *were* more than friends, but it's over. She broke things off before she left the wedding. Said she couldn't risk having feelings for me.'

Thiago frowned, looking as confused as Felipe felt. 'Sounds like she already has feelings for you, just like you have for her. She was probably just running scared.'

Felipe glanced at the floor, impotence a heavy weight on his shoulders. 'You've been married a day and you're already an expert on relationships?'

Thiago shrugged, nonplussed. 'I *am* an expert on some relationships. I know, for example, that you still have some warped big brother over-protective streak when it comes to me, and a sense of guilt because you didn't want to run Castillo Estates.'

Felipe pressed his lips together. He didn't want to have this conversation, least of all in a public place. But he couldn't let Thiago go on his honeymoon with this accusation unresolved.

'It wasn't your calling,' Thiago added before Felipe could interject. 'The rest of the family accepted that years ago. You're a much better doctor than you are a winemaker anyway. We're all proud of you. You're the only person who can't let it go. It's like you're scared to let yourself be happy again.'

Felipe shook his head. Having discussed it with Emilia, he had begun to let it go. She'd already pointed out his flawed thinking about his family. She'd given him a reason to question the status quo of his life. But Thiago was right. *Again*. Felipe had punished himself long enough for the things he saw as his failings.

'I *can* let it go,' he said, meeting Thiago's stare. 'And I'm proud of you and what you've achieved with the business. You're right. I wouldn't have been half as good as you at running the estate because it's not my passion.'

Thiago slapped Felipe's arm with enthusiasm. 'Whereas I'm excited by the challenges. I can't wait to watch my family grow up surrounded by the ancient vines. And Violetta feels the same way. It wasn't your calling but it's *ours.*'

Felipe nodded, his throat tight with emotion. Had he spent so long feeling guilty about his career choices and his failed marriage that he'd overlooked what made *him* excited? His career, for sure, but also someone to share all the good things in his life with. *Emilia.*

'But back to Emilia,' Thiago pressed. 'Did you tell her how you feel about her?'

'No.' Felipe winced, feeling stupid. 'I tried, but that just seemed to make things worse.' Because instead of telling her he had feelings for her, instead of telling her he'd fallen in love with her, he'd held back out of fear that he couldn't be what she needed, that he'd somehow let her down. Only now, it was so obvious. Even if she still didn't want him, even if she was still protecting her vulnerable heart, Emilia needed to know that he'd fallen head over heels in love with her anyway.

'So you let her run scared?' Thiago pointed out.

'Like I said, it's much more complicated second time around,' Felipe said, absolutely gutted that he'd allowed her to walk away without telling her how he felt. 'I was trying not to scare her off. She'll always love her husband, and I've no desire to make the same mistakes I did with Delfina.'

'Just because Emilia loves her husband doesn't

mean that she can't love you, too,' Thiago said, making it all sound so straightforward.

Felipe shook his head, speechless. Could Emilia love him back? Was that what she'd meant when she'd said *'before we both get our hearts broken'*? He needed to go to her—right now—and sort this out.

But Thiago hadn't finished. 'And you can't take all the blame for your divorce. I've heard that Delfina has moved on, so why can't you?'

'That's a great question.' Why couldn't he move on? Why was he punishing himself? Didn't he also deserve happiness?

As if he'd heard the unasked question, Thiago said, 'The family want to see you content, that's all. We love you. We want what's best for you, whatever that is. But don't let fear, either yours or Emilia's, stop you from being honest about your feelings. Tell her how you feel and what you want and take it from there.'

Felipe nodded, pulling Thiago in for one final hug. 'Thanks for the pep talk, little brother. Now go and enjoy your honeymoon. I have to go to Emilia.'

Because, just like Emilia, he *did* deserve to be happy. Only to achieve that he needed her. With a fresh sense of urgency, he grabbed his bag and took off running towards the taxi rank.

CHAPTER NINETEEN

A SUNDAY EVENING on the sofa with Eva watching a chick-flick was just what the doctor ordered. So Emilia jumped in surprise when the doorbell rang halfway through the film.

'I'll get it,' Eva said, pausing the movie. 'My friend Paloma said she might swing by.'

The dog jumped down from beside Emilia and followed Eva into the hall.

Seconds later, Eva called out, 'I'm just heading out to get some frozen yoghurt with Paloma. Don't wait up.'

What? That was sudden.

'Okay, *mija*,' Emilia called, feeling a little abandoned. She rose from the sofa and shuffled out to the hall to say goodbye.

'Felipe…' She gasped at the sight of him standing just inside the front door. He looked tired, a little rumpled, but wonderfully familiar, and Emilia's heart reached out to him. She'd hurt him last night and she needed to make it right.

Eva took her coat from the hook, winked at

her mother and pulled the door closed as she left. Emilia and Felipe were alone. For a few seconds they only stared at each other. Emilia held her breath, everything she wanted to say trapped in her throat by the surge of love she felt for this man.

'What are you doing here?' she finally asked, bewildered, her pulse fluttering with excitement. Then she remembered what she'd said and done yesterday and how she'd most likely already ruined her chances with him.

Felipe placed his overnight bag on the floor and stepped closer, his stare searching hers as if he was thinking of something to say. Emilia had a fleeting thought that perhaps she'd left something behind in Mendoza and he was simply there to return it. Her stomach sank, her second chance evaporating.

Then he reached for her hands. 'I'm sorry to come around uninvited, but I've been dying inside since you left yesterday.'

Fresh hope bloomed in her chest. 'I'm so sorry if I hurt you, Felipe.' She swallowed, her eyes smarting with tears that she'd caused him pain.

He shook his head, his stare growing more intense. 'It's my own fault,' he said with the passion that was a massive part of his personality. 'I was stupid enough to let you go last night, when I should have told you how I feel instead. I love you, Emilia.'

She gasped at his miraculous words, the floor tilting under her bare feet. Could that be true? Were his aunts right? Did he love her, after everything?

'I messed up,' he rushed on, his expression wreathed in sincerity, his vulnerability heartbreaking. 'I've always felt like I let my family down, and like I'd messed up my marriage, and I was scared that if I tried to have a relationship with you I'd only let you down, too. And I never, ever want to hurt you. There was so much more at stake for us, after everything you'd been through with Ricardo and with the added responsibility of Eva, who of course must always come first in your life.'

Too choked to speak, Emilia shook her head. There was finally space in her heart for love again—for *him*. He was just as important to her, too.

He released one of her hands and cupped her cheek, wiping away a tear she hadn't even known had escaped. 'But I'm not scared any more. You deserve to know how madly I've fallen in love with you, even if you can't love me back. I won't pressure you if you're not ready for a relationship, but I want to be in your life in any capacity you'll allow. To be there for you, always. As a friend and colleague if that's all you want, but I hope that one day you might want more...'

'Felipe…' Emilia released a sound, half sob, half exclamation of joy as she reached for him, her hands finding his waist. 'I was scared, too. But I *do* want more. I love you, too.'

'You do?' He frowned, staring so intently into her eyes it almost hurt to look at him.

'I do.' She nodded, tears spilling free.

He stepped closer, cupped her face in both hands and kissed her with fierce desperation. Emilia kissed him back, her heart soaring with love. He pulled back, holding her tightly as if he'd never again let her go—and that was fine with her. She was exactly where she wanted to be.

'I thought I was done with love after my marriage failed,' he said, pressing a kiss to her temple, 'but I was *so* wrong. I think I was scared to allow myself to be happy again, and I was obviously just waiting for *you*, wonderful you, without knowing it. Because you are everything I could ever want in a partner.'

Emilia looked up, blinking away the sting in her eyes. 'I'm so sorry I hurt you. I was scared that loving you meant I'd be betraying Ricardo, scared that I'd hurt Eva if I embarked on another relationship—although I'm sure that when she gets to know you she'll love you, too—scared that if I loved you as desperately as I do that I might lose you as well.'

He dragged her into his arms, pressing a kiss

to her forehead. 'I'm here. Nobody knows what's around the corner, but I'll love you fiercely and passionately for however long we have together. You are so beautiful. I want you to be mine. Always.'

No one could promise for ever. But the important thing was that they valued the time they did have together. That they squeezed every drop of life and love and joy from every day they shared. That they felt the fear and loved each other anyway.

Emilia held him tight. 'And I'll love you back the same way. I know it hasn't even been twenty-four hours since I left you, but I missed you so badly. You feel like home to me.' Taking his hand, she led him into the lounge and the sofa where they sat side by side, Luna content at their feet.

'I can't quite believe that you're here,' she said, caressing his handsome face. 'I had a long talk with Eva this morning, and I realised that you deserved to know how I felt. I was going to find you first thing tomorrow and beg you to give me another chance. I'm so sorry that I hurt you, that I allowed my fear to push you away when you've brought me back to life.'

Felipe gripped her hands, pressing kisses over her knuckles. 'And I'm sorry that I wasn't brave enough to fight for you at the wedding. Part of me knew that I loved you then, and I regret letting you leave without fully realising it.'

'But you're here now,' she whispered, her heart bursting with love for this thoughtful and passionate man who was everything she wanted and needed.

He nodded, pressing his lips to hers. 'I'm here now.'

Holding both her hands, he stared into her eyes—she saw his vulnerability. 'I wanted to ask you something. Don't freak out.'

Emilia laughed, kissed him, pulled back. 'Okay, I won't.'

'Will you date me—just me—exclusively?' His grip on her hands tightened. 'I'll make us work. I promise.'

'I will, absolutely.' She nodded, laughing through her tears. 'And *we'll* make us work.' She leaned in and kissed him again. She couldn't seem to stop and realised with a soaring heart that she didn't have to.

'In that case,' he said, his beaming smile lighting his eyes, 'How would you feel if we delete our dating apps together?'

Emilia gasped with excitement. 'I think that's a brilliant idea.' She reached for her phone and he pulled his from his pocket.

'Ready?' he asked, his finger poised over the icon on the screen.

'Definitely.' Emilia nodded, never more excited

to be rid of the horrible dating app. 'One, two, three.' They pressed the little x's in unison and the apps vanished back into the void.

'Good riddance,' Emilia said, her cheeks aching from smiling as she abandoned her phone and threw her arms around his neck. 'I only want *you*.' Her man, her friend, her lover.

'I only want *you*, for the rest of my life,' Felipe said, tossing aside his phone and reaching for Emilia, dragging her into his arms.

It wasn't a proposal, but it was a commitment nonetheless. A promise to be there for each other, with fully open hearts.

'And to think we met the old-fashioned way,' Emilia teased, her arms tight around the man she loved. How had she been so lucky to be given a second chance at love? To have met not one but two amazing men in her life.

'I am such a good dating coach,' he said playfully, his hands in her hair and his eyes full of love. 'I told you it would all work out.'

'You did and you were right,' she whispered, sinking into his kiss.

His lips caressed hers, their kisses growing more and more passionate. They loved each other all night long and Emilia finally had everything she needed.

EPILOGUE

Two years later...

THE CASTILLO ESTATE winery was even more spectacular in spring, the perfect season for a wedding celebration. Felipe once more stood under the antique wrought-iron gazebo with Thiago at his side, only this time *he* was the proud and nervous groom.

Only his nerves were more about excitement. After a long courtship—he'd asked Emilia to be his wife three months into their exclusive relationship—today he and Emilia would finally make it official.

The music began and Emilia emerged from the avenue of pink-blossomed Oleander trees that led back to the house. Felipe and Thiago had played under those very trees as boys, and to see the woman he loved in this magical place that was so close to his heart left him choked. He held his breath, his heart racing at the beautiful sight she made. Dressed in a simple sleeveless gold satin dress, with her hair casually pinned up, she looked breathtaking. Eva, wearing a deep blue dress, walked arm in arm at her mother's side.

His eyes met Emilia's, the small congregation of friends and family melting away for a second so they were alone in this intensely personal moment. Today was just about them and the love they'd found while neither of them had been searching.

Felipe grinned, the broad smile on his face impossible to stop. He probed his feelings, relieved to find no trace of the fear that had held him back for years. His relationship with Emilia wasn't perfect. They'd had their tests and trials over the past two years, like any couple. But every day they woke up together and showed up for their relationship, willing to work at it, to stay committed and to act with the unstoppable love and passion they shared.

When she reached his side, Felipe took her hand, leaning down to press a brief kiss on her lovely lips. 'I love you,' he whispered. 'You're beautiful.'

'Me too,' she replied, laughing as family members cheered at their sneaky pre-vow kiss.

But neither of them cared. Today was *their* day, a day of love, and the celebration of two families—one big and one small—coming together.

Felipe held Emilia's hand throughout the entire

ceremony, his heart swelling with so much love he thought it might burst. As they exchanged vows, promising to love and care for each other, he'd never felt more content or more certain of them as a couple. Of his ability to care for this woman and her daughter, and to make Emilia happy.

'Emilia and Felipe are now husband and wife,' the celebrant declared to raucous cheering from the audience.

Felipe held Emilia's face, slowly dipping his head to hers and bringing their lips together. Thoroughly and passionately he savoured their first kiss as a married couple. Emilia sank into his arms, her hands gripping his neck as she kissed him back with equal passion.

Kissing Emilia should never be rushed. Kissing his wife, likewise.

'I love you,' he said when he pulled back, staring down into her beautiful deep brown eyes. 'I'm never letting you go again.' He squeezed her hand to prove his point and she laughed.

'I love you, too.' She smiled that secret smile of hers and his heart soared.

Second time around wasn't without its challenges, but the rewards when you made that commitment were magnified tenfold. He and Emilia would cherish every moment they had together— a little older, hopefully a little wiser, but no less in love.

As they were swallowed up by well-wishers, engulfed in hugs and kisses and congratulations, Felipe kept his promise and kept a hold of his wife's hand.

As the entire wedding party moved to the barn, which was festooned with swathes of romantic flower garlands and twinkling lights, Emilia couldn't seem to stop smiling. With Eva at her side as maid of honour, and Felipe holding on tightly to her hand, she felt cocooned in love.

'It's so beautiful,' Emilia whispered to Felipe as everyone poured into the barn and the party began—the wine flowing, the music playing and their loved ones smiling.

Felipe motioned to a waiter, who handed them each a glass of special sparkling wine, a vintage that had been specifically created by Thiago for Emilia and Felipe's wedding. It even had their names on the label.

'A toast, just for us, before the partying begins,' Felipe said, touching his glass to hers. 'To you my beautiful wife. May our marriage be long and full of passion. I will love you and take care of you and Eva every day of my life.'

'And to you, my dashing husband.' She smiled, blinking away the sting in her eyes as she stared at him over the rim of her glass. 'I'll love you and support you and care for you and our marriage with all of my heart, always.'

They both took a sip of the delicious wine and then Felipe drew her into his arms, kissing her once more. Emilia melted into the kiss, indulging in her husband's lips for far longer than was decent. But she didn't care. Life was too short to deny yourself the good things it had to offer.

When they pulled apart there was another cheer from the guests, punctuated by the odd wolf-whistle and cry of, *'Get a room!'*

Felipe dipped his head to whisper, 'All in good time.'

His promise for their wedding night sent shivers down Emilia's spine. But she forced herself to act with decorum and welcome her guests. She and Felipe worked the room hand in hand, stopping for a chat with each friend and family member in turn. By the time they reached their work colleagues from the General their glasses had been refilled several times.

'I hear you're both going to be working part-time when you return from your honeymoon,' Isabella Lopez said, her husband Sebastian at her side. The triplets—Sergio, Lorenzo and a happy and healthy Luis—were toddling around, kept safe with the helping hands of their friends from the hospital and nearby clinic, Carlos, Sofia, Gabriel and Ana.

'We are,' Felipe confirmed, his arm around Emilia's waist, holding her close. 'We have too much life to enjoy living to work full-time. I don't want the hospital to be the only place I see my wife.'

Emilia smiled up at him, excitement for their future a flutter in her veins. With Eva in her penultimate year at law school and living in a flat with her uni friends, she and Felipe had sold Emilia's house and moved in together to Felipe's apartment. There was a spare room for Eva, if she ever needed it, and Luna and Dante kept each other company, enjoying daily walks with the dogwalker while they were at the hospital.

Life was good again, and Emilia would never take one second of it for granted.

Later that night, after the best party ever, Felipe swung her up into his arms and carried her over the threshold of the estate's guest house.

'Congratulations, Mrs Castillo,' he said as he kicked the door closed and placed her on her feet, making sure that her body slid down his so her every nerve was electrified.

'Congratulations, husband,' she said, undoing the top few buttons of his shirt to press kisses to his chest, his jaw, his smiling lips.

'Now, stop talking,' she said, taking his hand and dragging him to the bedroom.

And he did.

* * * * *

*If you missed the previous story in the
Buenos Aires Docs quartet, then check out*

Daring to Fall for the Single Dad Doc
by Becky Wicks

*And if you enjoyed this story, check out
these other great reads from JC Harroway*

Her Secret Valentine's Baby
Phoebe's Baby Bombshell
Breaking the Single Mom's Rules

All available now!

Reader Service

Enjoyed your book?

Try the perfect subscription for Romance readers and get more great books like this delivered right to your door.

See why over 10+ million readers have tried Harlequin Reader Service.

Start with a Free Welcome Collection with free books and a gift—valued over $20.

Choose any series in print or ebook. See website for details and order today:

TryReaderService.com/subscriptions

RSBPA24R